Fastball

Edited by Michelle Josette
FictionEdit.com

ISBN-10: 1981137858
ISBN-13: 978-1981137855

Fastball

A Financial Thriller

PHILIP BECK

To my family and friends for providing me
encouragement to write this book.

PROLOGUE

Wendy Heygood was a good person. She didn't have to die that way. Her brutal murder shocked all of us. Up until the end, she led the good life fueled by her estranged husband Jack's fraudulent real estate company that no longer existed. Most of the money was gone but not forgotten by the disgruntled investors who lost everything.

Several years ago, I thought I knew Jack and Wendy well. Now I don't know. Over the course of the summer baseball season their story started to unravel and I learned about unethical behavior, questionable business dealings, illicit sexual relationships and murder that resulted from unsavory deeds.

CHAPTER 1

Tropical Investments, Inc., a vast real estate investment empire, headquartered in West Palm Beach, Florida with extensive holdings across the country and the Caribbean, filed for bankruptcy protection two years ago. The bankruptcy court examiner and the FBI later determined that a small cabal of insiders had orchestrated a Ponzi scheme and defrauded investors out of hundreds of millions of dollars. People's life savings vanished. All of the Tropical Investments insiders are now in federal prison except for my friend Jack Heygood. Jack's job as Senior Vice President of Marketing was to attract investors and raise capital to fund the firm's growth and investments. He was the "money guy" and a consummate salesman. His commanding presence instilled confidence in investors, coupled with a disarming style that made people feel at ease. Jack's favorite saying is "It's all in the presentation!" Numerous shareholder lawsuits were filed and the investors are demanding blood but there is no sign of Jack.

Summer baseball brought Jack, his wife, Wenduo "Wendy" Wang Heygood, and me together. Our boys have played baseball on the same summer teams for the last ten years. Jack and I coached for the first few years until we realized how little we knew about baseball and that the boys would be better served by professional coaching. Wendy Heygood is in her early forties and one of the top-producing real estate agents in Dallas with a quick wit, charismatic personality and a dynamite figure. Many of the dads on the team occasionally glance at her out of the corner of their eye during the games. She strikes me as a very confident woman who always gets exactly what she wants. I consider her to be a good friend. Wendy and her husband Jack met as undergraduates in Austin over twenty years ago and have been together ever since. However, Jack is now shrouded in mystery.

I last broke bread with Wendy and Jack Heygood two years ago. I had been reviewing reports in my office at National Airlines and my cell phone rang. It was Wendy Heygood. "Lonny, it's been a long time, how are you and Joe doing?" and Wendy added, "Jack is flying in from New York this afternoon and we plan to eat dinner at *Pedro's* in Snyder Plaza. Would you be interested in joining us?"

"I love the swirl margaritas with sangria, and the chicken enchiladas are outstanding. Sounds like a great idea! What time?"

"It's a date, see you at six," said Wendy.

Pedro's was at the north end of Snyder Plaza and there were no close parking spots available when I arrived at 5:45 p.m. I circled the plaza three times and finally found a parking spot four blocks to the south. It was a five-minute walk to *Pedro's* past the stylish boutiques. I waited outside to meet Jack and Wendy.

The whining from the engine of Wendy's Porsche announced her arrival. Just as she reached the front of *Pedro's* a lady in a Mercedes backed out and opened up a parking spot that Wendy immediately occupied. I laughed and thought to myself that the seas always seemed to part for Wendy no matter what the situation.

Wendy exited her car and walked over to me. As usual, she looked perfect, like a Neiman Marcus model, and had a big smile on her face. Wendy stood 5'7" and weighed around 115 pounds with shoulder-length black hair. She wore a white blouse and black pants. A gold necklace hung from her neck. Wendy gave me a hug and we went inside the restaurant to talk before Jack arrived. We walked past the long bar on the right with four televisions mounted behind it, all tuned to sports channels, and sat in a booth towards the back of the restaurant underneath a colorful painting of Jerry Jeff Walker. Three businessmen occupied the table to our left and appeared to be in an intense negotiation. Four sorority girls sat in the booth behind us and looked like they had been drinking for some time. Wendy smiled at me and started to talk.

"I was sorry to hear that you and Joan split up. How are you and Joe doing?"

"The divorce is final," I told her. "Joan didn't fight me for custody of Joe, in fact, she didn't want it. Joan wanted to move forward with her boss, I mean boyfriend, and not have anything tie her down."

Wendy took a sip of water from her glass and looked at me for several moments before finally saying, "That's so sad to hear, Lonny."

"Yeah, she wasn't interested in the house or her kid and just wanted her share of our estate in cash. Her boyfriend is not much of a father figure and is not interested in having to deal with a fifteen-year-old in his house."

To shift the uncomfortable conversation away from my ex-wife and failed marriage, I asked, "Well, what about you and Jack?"

Wendy leaned back and smiled. "My real estate business is very profitable and I enjoy the work. Jack's company has been great to us. The compensation is outstanding and enabled us to do many new things."

"I like your Porsche Targa 4s; it is beautiful, what's the color?" I asked.

"The Targa is Sapphire Blue Metallica," Wendy responded with a smile.

"Do you remember when we were both driving Civics?" I said with a laugh.

Wendy grimaced, rolled her eyes and then smiled politely. "Lonny, that was a long time ago, before I became successful."

We looked up and saw that Jack had arrived and spotted us. Jack was tall, around 6'2", with brown hair, a dark complexion and deep-set dark eyes that were accentuated by his gray pinstriped Brooks Bros. suit. He was usually the energetic and ebullient sales guy but today he looked tired and subdued. Jack's eyes darted from side to side as he sat down next to Wendy and across the table from me.

"Jack, good to see you, how was your flight?" I asked.

"We waited sixty minutes on the ground at LaGuardia before we took off. The pilot said there was an FAA delay program on the East Coast."

Jack shifted in his seat, laid his napkin on his lap and glanced across the table.

"Yeah, I know. National's on-time performance took a hit today. Well, glad you finally made it home."

Jack nodded in agreement. "Lonny, what would you like to drink? How about if we start off with a pitcher of margaritas? I remember how much you like them here at *Pedro's*!"

"Great idea! The swirl margaritas are the best in Dallas."

The waiter arrived, took our drink order and the pitcher of margaritas was on the way. Jack's eyes opened wide and then he paused and looked at me for a few seconds. "How's life at National Airlines?"

I took a sip of water. "My team just finished pricing out a jet engine deal and we are supporting the negotiations with the ground workers."

"Didn't you tell me six months ago that your group was going to expand beyond financial analysis and planning?" asked Jack.

"I added an analytics function. We do a lot of forecasting and optimization now in addition to the financial work," I said. "So how was your trip to New York?"

The smile left Jack's face as he leaned forward. "I just spent the week meeting with our investors in New York City. Investor confidence in Tropical has been negatively impacted by the unfair reports of our difficulties in the financial press and we needed to do a road show and communicate directly to our investors."

I grabbed a chip from the basket, dipped it in the red sauce and looked up at Jack. "How did those investor meetings go?"

Jack took a deep breath. "For the most part, the meetings went well. I wasn't able to attract new investment but the majority of people were happy to keep their current investment positions."

I squeezed the juice from the lime into my frozen margarita and took a sip. "I heard one investor complain to a reporter on a business TV channel that he was told he couldn't liquidate his investment in Tropical."

"Well, maybe that's true in a few rare occasions but it's not the norm," said Jack as his hands tightened into fists.

"Jack, how do you think Tropical Investments is doing?" I asked.

Jack usually liked to engage in snappy repartee when we talked about our jobs but paused for a moment with a blank expression on his face before he started to speak. "Well...huh...I don't—"

Wendy interrupted with a hand on his arm. "Tropical had a momentary setback and will return to profitability soon."

Jack looked like he wanted to say something but remained silent with Wendy's hand still on his arm. Wendy and Jack exchanged glances and there was an awkward moment of silence.

The conversation was starting to get uncomfortable so I decided to change the subject.

"Tell me about your new home on Strait Lane."

Wendy's eyes gleamed and she gave a half smile. "Construction was just completed and we moved in last month. The landscaping is still in progress and it will probably be another month before we have people over. We want you and Joe to visit soon."

Her comment amused me since I was last invited to their home four years ago. But their new home on Strait Lane interested me and I wanted to hear more about it.

"That estate must be quite the investment!"

"We paid two and a half million for the property and tore down the existing house built in the 1950s. Construction of our new house cost over one million. With the real estate market in Dallas, we could probably flip it today for four or five million," Wendy explained matter-of-factly.

"Do you have any celebrity neighbors?" I asked.

"Several as a matter of fact, but all great people." Wendy laughed, adding, "Sometimes the helicopters wake me up."

We finished the first pitcher of margaritas and ordered dinner. All three of us chose the very tasty chicken enchiladas. Another pitcher of margaritas followed as we reminisced about our many previous baseball summers together. After an hour we finished dinner and walked outside to briefly talk on the sidewalk near Wendy's Porsche. "Lonny, it's been great to catch up," Wendy said. "I hope to see you and Joe over at our house soon."

Then she excused herself and backed the Porsche out of the parking spot. Soon we could hear the whining of her high-performance engine as she drove off. Jack had parked near me at the other end of Snyder Plaza so we had a chance to continue our conversation as we walked to our cars. Jack and I had been pretty close years ago so I wondered how he was really doing.

"Jack, you were kind of quiet tonight, is everything okay?"

Jack grimaced and briefly shut his eyes. "I am under a tremendous amount of pressure at Tropical as we try to work our way through this tough spot. Life is much more complicated and not as much fun as it was when we coached the boys in the rec league six years ago."

We walked a couple of blocks and were now standing in front of my high-performance, Dark Highland Green, 2008 Mustang GT *Bullitt* special edition so the conversation was going to end soon.

Jack studied my car for a few seconds. "Lonny, I see you're still driving the old *Bullitt.* Is the paint job new?"

"Nope, just had it buffed up after a fender-bender on 183."

"Lonny, you need to slow down…and stop trying to drive like Steve McQueen." Jack paused for a moment and continued. "Well, I need to get going. It was a pleasure to see you and catch up. Be safe."

"Jack, if you ever want to go out for a beer and talk, please give me a call," I said.

We shook hands and then Jack continued to walk south towards his car as I sat down in the *Bullitt.* After taking a couple of steps, Jack turned and motioned me to lower the window.

"Did you ever replace that cheap, after-market muffler?"

"Yeah, with original equipment re-piped per factory specs."

A smile came to Jack's face. "Crank it."

I started the car and revved the engine. A gurgling rumble filled the air…and could be felt in the *Bullitt.* Jack nodded and gave me a thumbs-up.

Then he turned and continued to walk south to his car. I pulled out and started the short drive home. I was a little bit disconcerted by our conversation. Hopefully, better times were ahead for Jack Heygood.

• • •

Three weeks later I was sitting at the kitchen table in my BVDs and reading the business section of the Dallas paper over breakfast when I saw a headline on page three stating that a large Florida-based real estate company, Tropical Investments, Inc., filed for Chapter 11 bankruptcy protection in federal court. The lives of Wendy and Jack Heygood would never be the same again.

CHAPTER 2

Coaches Ronny Espinosa and Stan White will lead the 17U (ages seventeen and under) Dallas Generals baseball team this summer. Coach Ronny is thirty-five years old and was born and bred in California's Central Valley. Ronny's parents were migrant farm workers who eventually settled in Bakersfield, California. He stands a little under 5'10" with dark skin and a pencil-thin mustache. Coach Ronny earned all-conference honors as a second baseman at a small, Division II college in California and later played for three years in the Mexican League. He was never able to break into the minor leagues because of his below-average hitting skills. Coach Stan is six feet tall and probably weighs around 200 pounds. He was a junior college All-American and played four years in the Dodgers organization, advancing to AA before being released. Both Ronny and Stan have coached select baseball teams in Dallas for several summers. They are at the house tonight to offer Joe a spot on the Generals.

Coaches Ronny and Stan arrived promptly at 7pm and I answered the door and showed them inside. "Guys, thanks for coming over to the house tonight," I said as we sat down in the living room. Stan and Ronny sat on the couch while Joe and I sat directly across the coffee table from them in matching chairs. I had never seen the coaches without their hats and sunglasses on so I was somewhat surprised to see Stan's thinning, blond hair combed straight back and the large bald spot on the back of Ronny's head. Stan had a square face with a very large jaw while Ronny had beady eyes that danced back and forth.

Ronny glanced at Joe and me. "Mike Rizzo wanted to be here too but he's stuck in California on business."

"He's a coaching legend here in Dallas. Will he be involved with the team this year?" I asked.

"Mike has been splitting his time between Dallas and Pacific Palisades since his business expanded to California. He's the general manager and should help to coach in the National Championship Tournament (NCT) during early August in Phoenix," said Stan.

"Have you put the roster together?" I asked.

Ronny took a drink of his soda and looked at Joe. "We're still trying to fill a few spots but have a real good group so far."

"It's a real mix of backgrounds; we plan to have three kids on scholarship," said Stan.

"Our goal is the NCT, that's what this season is all about. We need to get there and win, it's the big enchilada," said Ronny.

Stan nodded in agreement and his expression

hardened. "We don't have a participation-trophy mentality. If we're not one of the top ten teams in the country and make the NCT then our season is a total failure."

"All of the elite programs from across the country participate in the NCT," I said.

"Yeah, Mike got a call from the East Cobb, Georgia manager a couple of days ago; they are real good and look forward to kicking our butts," said Ronny with a laugh. "We always play in their tournament in Atlanta in June and usually see them again at the NCT."

"The Cincinnati program is always good. They recruit nationally and have even called some players in Texas," said Stan.

Ronny scratched at his mustache. "We don't have that kind of budget; we just recruit in Texas and Oklahoma."

"Lonny, could you and Joe host an out-of-town player?" inquired Stan.

"That's okay with me—Joe, what do you think?"

"Fine with me," Joe said. "He could hang out with Mark Heygood and me."

"Joe, you're one of our top recruits. Most of the college scouts have you high on their list of pitchers," said Ronny. "We consider Heygood and you to be a package deal. If you come, we'll take Heygood."

Stan added, "The feedback from the college scouts is that they think you can throw five different pitches with command for strikes and that you run like a deer. You project at the next level. In their minds, you could be both a position player in the outfield and pitch."

"But don't get us wrong about Heygood," Ronny said. "He has a nice bat with some power but the mobility is limited; we don't have many options where we could line him up defensively."

"Yeah, Heygood is a good kid," said Stan.

Ronny grinned. "Besides, his mother Wendy is easy on the eyes."

My eyes shifted to Stan as he frowned and shook his head disapprovingly.

"So Joe, what do you think about playing for the Generals?" asked Stan.

Joe nodded. "I'm all in with the Generals, looking forward to the season."

"You have made a good decision; the college scouts want me to send them a copy of our schedule so you will get a lot of visibility. I expect plenty of the MLB teams will scout us too since the draft is just a year away," said Ronny.

"You mentioned that a couple of roster spots haven't been filled. Who are you looking at?" I asked.

A big smile appeared on Ronny's face. "Have you heard of Josh Baker?"

"Oh yeah, Josh is the super athlete from Lubbock who plays football and baseball."

"Yes, he has breakaway speed on the football field and would look good in center field," said Ronny. "Sort of a white Bo Jackson."

"He throws left-handed and his fastball touches 95 mph," added Stan. "He's the kind of player who could be a difference maker in the NCT."

Stan paused and raised his hands palms up from the coffee table. "However, their family situation is a mess. Butch, Josh's father, did a stretch in the state prison in Huntsville for assault and battery, and the mother enlisted in the Army several years ago and is out of the picture."

"From what I gather, Josh has to take care of

himself most of the time," said Ronny.

Joe leaned back in his chair. "Is Josh interested in playing baseball with the Generals?"

"I think so but it's hard to tell who's calling the shots. I've had a couple of conversations with Butch and I haven't figured him out. It seems like he's trying to work some angle," Ronny said.

"If we can get Josh to play, I would like him to stay with you guys here in Dallas," said Stan.

"Fine with us," I agreed.

"Great, Ronny and I will be in touch about the preseason practice schedule at the end of the high school baseball season."

The conversation ended and the coaches stood to leave. I was relieved that Joe had secured a spot on the best 17U baseball team in Dallas.

CHAPTER 3

The phone was ringing as I walked through the back door of my house after a long day at National Airlines. The caller ID displayed my ex-wife's number. God, did I want to talk to her? She had moved out a few years ago and was shacking up with her boss. The marriage lasted fifteen years but we were just going through the motions for the last five. At forty-five, Joan is starting to show her age with wrinkles around her eyes and some added weight. Back in the day she was a vivacious blonde bombshell with a naughty smile. The kind of woman you might want to take to Las Vegas for a long weekend but not the kind of person you marry. After a couple more rings, I picked up.

"Hello, this is Lonny," I announced.

"Lonny, this is Joan, put Joe on."

Joan's cold tone did not surprise me.

"Nice to hear from you, I am doing great," I responded.

"Where's Joe?"

"Our son is at the Heygoods' house playing catch with Mark."

"What are you thinking?"

"Huh?"

"You let Joe go to the Heygoods'?"

"What's the problem? Mark is playing on Joe's summer baseball team."

"Jack Heygood should be in prison with the rest of the Tropical Investments execs. How many millions of dollars did he steal?"

"We were friends with Jack and Wendy."

"Jack is a crook. Wendy had to know what was going on. I never liked her."

"Have you called Joe's cell?"

"No answer."

"When he gets home, I'll tell him you called."

"Lonny, I might as well let you know, Hal and I are going to Europe in June and we want Joe to come with us."

"That's just great. So after three years, your boyfriend finally wants to spend some time with our son. I hate to break the bad news but Joe is playing ball with the Dallas Generals and the season runs through early August."

"Does Joe even want to play or are you still trying to live your life through him?"

"Of course he does, Joe is one of the best pitchers in Texas and he can showcase his talents in front of the college scouts."

"Good grief."

"The Generals are the top 17U select team in Dallas. Playing with them will open a lot of doors. The colleges have started to recruit him. Maybe you should show a little interest in his activities and see him play."

"Lonny, let Joe make his own decisions. You have been pushing him into baseball since he was seven years old."

"What? That's ridiculous."

"How many kids that age have a pitching mound and batting cage in the backyard?"

"Joe is focused and wants to let baseball take him as far as possible."

"Well, I hope you are now more under control."

"What's that supposed to mean?"

"Everyone on the block knows what happened when you threw batting practice to Joe after he got home late from a party last month. You woke up the neighbors and yelled at them when they asked you to stop."

"If Joe wants to do BP then we are doing BP. Screw the neighbors. Ask me if I care what they think."

"Lonny, just tell Joe to give me a call."

"Sure, Joan." I hung up.

● ● ●

My best friend, Maggie Ross, lives three doors down the street. Although in her mid-forties, she still has her tall, lean cross-country build from college, with shoulder-length brown hair and blue eyes. Maggie lost her husband to cancer two years ago and is still grieving the loss. Her marriage, unlike mine, had been a happy and fulfilling relationship that produced two grown daughters. We get together two to three times a week after work to enjoy a glass of wine or Diet Coke, discuss a wide range of topics from politics to home repair and enjoy each other's company. Maggie is witty and has a great sense of humor. We often finish each other's sentences. She is Director of Accounting at a large pizza chain and we get some laughs swapping work stories. Even though we're pals, Maggie never comes to the house without calling as she doesn't want to disrupt a visit from a female guest. Some of my buddies have suggested that Maggie might be an ideal mate for me but, so far, we are still just friends.

I looked at my watch shortly after ending the call with Joan—it was almost 6:30. Maggie said she'd be here by now and the conversation with Joan prevented me from picking up the house so I hurried to address the big issues. Then I heard the doorbell and opened the door. There was Maggie standing on my front porch grinning. "Maggie, nice to see you, come on in."

"Lonny, how was your day?"

"Great until about twenty minutes ago when my ex called."

We walked into the kitchen and sat down. Maggie nodded and said, "Sorry to hear that."

"She was upset that Joe is over at the Heygoods' house."

Maggie shifted in her chair. "Why? Mark Heygood seems like a nice kid; what's the story with that?"

"Well, Jack Heygood used to work for Tropical Investments, the company that failed two years ago. He probably should be in jail."

The smile left Maggie's face. "Where is he?"

"Nobody seems to know. It's like he dropped off the face of the earth after the other Tropical execs were put on trial and convicted."

Maggie scrunched up her face. "Tropical was based in Palm Beach, Florida but his family is here in Dallas?"

"Yeah, Jack and Wendy Heygood have lived in Dallas for the last twenty years. She's still in the house on Strait Lane with their son Mark. When Jack worked for Tropical it didn't matter where he lived. He was a road warrior and met with investors across the country."

"Lonny, the Heygoods are a bit of a question mark. I guess I can see why Joan was apprehensive."

I poured Maggie and me a glass of merlot and we walked into the living room and sat on the couch near the coffee table. The smile reappeared on her face so I wondered what was up.

"Enough about Jack Heygood and Joan," I said. "How are things going with you?"

"We started the April accounting close yesterday so I am pretty busy."

"How are the girls?"

"They're doing great. It's nice that they're now both in Houston with their husbands and can see each other."

"Jennifer lives near Rice and the zoo, right? What about Mary?"

"Mary is just south of the Katy Freeway off of Kirkwood."

"That's an easy drive on the weekend."

Maggie paused for a moment. "Mary told me today that she's pregnant."

"Oh, so that's why you can't stop smiling. That's great, congratulations!"

Maggie looked thrilled and sat there beaming on the couch next to me. I leaned in and briefly gave her a hug.

"This is cause for celebration; let me throw a couple of steaks on the grill."

Maggie reached out and touched my hand. "Thank you, Lonny. That sounds perfect."

I started the gas grill on my patio as Maggie opened another bottle of merlot. It was still early with plenty of time for us to talk. We were on our second glasses by the time I started cooking the steaks. In a few minutes Maggie went inside to fix the salad and sauté the mushrooms while I flipped the steaks on the grill. The meat had a nice aroma as it sizzled on the top rack.

"Lonny, the meat smells great," said Maggie, stepping outside. "You're a fantastic cook."

"Thank you very much. This is a special day for your family. I'm glad we could celebrate."

Maggie just looked at me and smiled.

"What do your daughter and son-in-law plan to name the baby?"

With a laugh, she said, "Well, they are considering several names but they won't tell me which ones."

I took the steaks off the grill and placed them on a large plate that I would use to carry them into the kitchen. Maggie poured us another round of merlot as we sat down at the kitchen table and started to consume the tasty steaks and salad. We finished eating in twenty minutes and then I washed the dishes while she dried them.

"Lonny, this was fantastic, thank you very much."

I smiled and walked with her to the door. "Thank you for coming over and sharing the great news. Good night, Maggie."

CHAPTER 4

Several weeks after my meeting with the coaches, I was in the middle of a budget meeting in my office at National Airlines. Then the phone rang. It was Coach Ronny Espinosa. "Lonny, I've talked to Josh's dad, Butch, on a couple of occasions about Josh playing with the Generals this summer but he still hasn't committed. Since you and Joe will be Josh's host family, could you give Butch a call and help with the recruitment?"

"Sure Coach, I would be happy to."

Later that evening after I had returned home and fixed dinner for Joe, I placed a call to Butch in Lubbock. "Hello Mr. Baker, this is Lonny Jones. My son Joe plays on the Dallas Generals and we want to host Josh this summer in Dallas. "

"Lonny, I appreciate the call. Ronny Espinosa told me to expect your call," said Butch in a slurred voice. "I would like to meet you personally to talk about Josh and the Generals. Could you come out to

Lubbock so we could talk?"

"Sure, I could come to your house early on Saturday morning."

Flying to Lubbock was not a big deal since I worked for National Airlines and could fly for a small fee if there was space available on the airplane. I drove to Dallas/Fort Worth Airport (DFW) early on Saturday and boarded the first National Airlines flight to Lubbock. It was early and I was very tired from the grueling workweek so I went to sleep as soon as the jet lifted off the ground. I was awakened by the flight attendant's announcement to fasten seat belts ten minutes before landing. I had never visited Lubbock before so I looked out the window to catch a glimpse of the scenery. My first reaction was that we must be landing on the moon as all I saw was rock and sand. The landing was smooth and I deplaned and headed to the rental car desk. Soon I was driving south on I27 towards Lubbock and Butch's house. Coach Ronny Espinosa had told me that Butch had served time in the state prison in Huntsville but was now employed and back on his feet.

Butch's modest house was located south of campus in the 3500 block of 25th Street just off of Joliet Avenue. The small, gray house with white trim looked like it was built in the early 1950s. The grass was cut short but I noticed several different shades of green so it looked like the turf was a mixture of grass and weeds. I pulled up and parked the rental car in front of the house on the street. No cars were in the driveway and there didn't seem to be any activity at the house. I got out of the car and walked up the driveway to the front door. The garage door was up and I noticed a weight bench and several 45-pound weights on the floor. I knocked but no one answered. After a few minutes, I started to walk back to my rental car and wondered what to do next. Just as I reached the street, a young, shirtless man opened the door and emerged from the house. I turned, took one look at him and knew it was Josh Baker. He looked exactly like how Coach Espinosa described him. He was an athlete: crew cut, 5'11" and 215 pounds with bulging muscles in a V-shaped torso—which was either a gift from God or a product of a chemistry experiment.

I walked back to the front door. "Good morning Josh, I'm Lonny Jones from Dallas. Butch asked me to meet him this morning to talk about summer baseball and the Generals. Have you seen him today?"

Josh extended his hand. "Nice to meet you, Mr. Jones. I heard you were coming to Lubbock. Coach Espinosa told me you guys would be my host family this summer."

"My son Joe is looking forward to playing ball with you."

"I saw Joe pitch in a tournament in Austin. He looked pretty good."

"I appreciate that very much, Josh. I've read several articles about your season—you've put up great numbers all year. I think you would enjoy staying with us in Dallas this summer. I'd like to talk with your dad to answer any questions he might have about the Generals or you staying with us."

The smile disappeared from Josh's face. "The police came here to the house last night. My dad was arrested."

I was stunned and didn't know what to say. The silence lasted several seconds. "May I ask why Butch was arrested?"

"The police said he beat someone up after a card game yesterday afternoon. Butch tried to explain to the police that it was all a misunderstanding but they didn't want to listen. He's in the Lubbock Sheriff's Jail downtown on Main Street."

"Sorry to hear that, Josh. Here's my contact information in Dallas. Joe and I would be happy to talk to you any time about the upcoming season." Then I handed him a National Airlines business card with Joe's cell and our house numbers written on the back.

I returned to the rental car and tried to determine what I should do next. Since I was in Lubbock, why not try to visit Butch in jail? It was a long shot but why not give it a try? I started driving northeast towards downtown.

I pulled up in front of the jail and fortunately, since it was Saturday morning, downtown Lubbock was empty and there were plenty of parking spaces available. The jail was a five-floor, brownish building adjacent to the sheriff's office. I walked in and headed to the booking desk. Standing in front of the booking officer, I asked, "I understand that Butch Baker is an inmate in the jail. I came to Lubbock to visit him this morning and learned he was arrested. Can I visit him today?"

"No, visiting hours are over for today," responded the officer from behind the very thick safety glass window. "You could visit him at the county jail on Sunday."

"That's not going to work. I need to return to Dallas this afternoon."

"Well, his lawyer Nick Del Monico offices across the street. Could he help you?"

"Thanks, Officer," I said as I started to walk out of the jail and back to my car parked in front.

This trip was not going as expected and I was ready to punt and head back to Preston Smith International Airport and fly home. I was getting into the rental car and looked up and saw that I had parked directly in front of Nick Del Monico's office. What the heck, I would give this a shot.

The law office was in a one-story building adjacent to a couple of bail bonds outfits. I walked in the front door and was greeted by his secretary. She was a small pleasant-looking woman with a warm smile. The office walls had Western art displayed and appeared to be much more casual than the law offices I had frequented in downtown Dallas.

"Is Mr. Del Monico in today?"

Before she could answer I heard, "Yes, I am. How can I help you?" Nick emerged from the back office wearing a gray pinstriped suit. He was a tall man—at least 6'3"—in his early 60s, with a tanned, weather-beaten face and blondish-brown hair with a touch of gray above his ears.

"I am Lonny Jones from Dallas. I came to Lubbock today to talk with your client Butch Baker about his son playing summer baseball in Dallas this summer. He said he had some questions and wanted to talk."

A wry smile appeared on Nick's face. "Oh, I know all about it. Please step into my office."

Nick's office was spacious with a large desk located towards the back of the room. A coffee table surrounded by two chairs and a couch sat in the middle of the room. The chairs and the couch were covered by tan, crushed natural leather and looked very comfortable. I noticed a wet bar on the far side of the room with a metal tray containing several shot glasses and a bottle of Wild Turkey. A very large, fully equipped golf bag leaned against the bar. "Please sit down, Mr. Jones. May I pour you an eye opener?" said Nick as he glanced to the wet bar.

"No, thank you, but a cup of coffee sounds good." Nick walked to the outer office and poured me a cup from the percolator near his secretary's desk.

"Mr. Del Monico, do you play a lot of golf?" I asked as Nick handed me the mug.

"Please call me Nick. Yes, I play the Rawls course at least twice a week."

We sat down in the very comfortable crushed-leather chairs and continued our earlier conversation. Nick's previous comment had surprised me. "You knew I was coming to Lubbock?"

Nick laughed and said, "Sure I did. Josh is a good kid but a little rough around the edges. With proper supervision and guidance he could be an asset to any baseball team. I know the Generals' coaches covet his skills." Nick continued. "The coaches, especially Ronny Espinosa, have said a lot of good things about Josh."

"His baseball skills could be showcased across the country this summer," I added, trying to highlight the benefits of Josh playing with the Generals.

"Mr. Jones, I could make it happen for Josh to play with the Generals for a thousand dollars."

I was stunned by Nick's proposal. "So Butch wanted me to come to Lubbock to negotiate the fee?" I asked.

Nick's expression turned devilish. "Yes, probably so."

"Well, I don't know anything about paying

players and I am certainly not going to write you a check today but I'll report back to Coach Espinosa when I return to Dallas."

"Pleasure doing business with you, Mr. Jones," said Nick as I walked out of his office. Just before I exited the outer office door onto the sidewalk, Nick called out, "Lonny, I have an extra set of clubs and a noon tee time at the Rawls course, care to join me?"

"Thank you, Nick, but I need to catch an early flight back to Dallas," I said as I waved goodbye.

It was only 10:30 a.m. and I already had a throbbing headache. I drove through a Mexican restaurant on 19th Street that was highly recommended by friends who went to college in Lubbock. After washing down a burrito with coffee, I headed back to the airport hoping to catch the noon flight back to Dallas. I wondered if Coach Espinosa knew what Butch wanted to talk to me about. Did the coach expect me to negotiate a deal and write a check?

My return flight to Dallas landed on time and I checked my phone messages. There was only one: "Hi Lonny, this is Maggie. I have a plumbing problem in my kitchen, please call me."

I had Maggie on the phone momentarily. "Hi Maggie, I just landed at DFW, what's going on?"

"There's a leak in the kitchen sink. I can't get the water to stop."

"Where's the leak? Is it at the base of the spout or is water coming out from the end of the spout?"

"When I turn the water on, it leaks at the base of the spout and when I turn it off it leaks from the end of the spout."

"It's a Delta faucet, right?"

"Yes, I think so."

"Okay, I'll stop by Bivins Brothers plumbing supply company on the way to your house and get new O rings for the base and new springs and seats to stop the flow out of the end of the spout."

Thirty minutes later I arrived at Maggie's house with the plumbing supplies in hand, pulled my toolbox out of the back of the Mustang and knocked on the back door. Maggie opened the door with a grin on her face. "Hi Lonny, thanks for helping me. How much do I owe you for parts?"

"No problem, how about you bring the wine next time we get together?" I joked and added, "Sometimes I think you only see me because you want to have an on-call plumber two doors down!"

I turned off the water under the sink, disassembled the faucet and replaced the parts. The repair was complete in ten minutes. We sat down at Maggie's kitchen table and enjoyed a cold glass of iced tea. Maggie's eyes widened. "So, how was your trip to Lubbock today?"

"It is a long, strange story. The person I wanted to talk to is in jail. But I did speak to his attorney."

"Huh."

"You will not believe this."

"What?"

"The dad and his lawyer want to be paid for letting the boy play for the Generals this summer."

"Wow, that's crazy. You always said some of the select baseball parents are real characters."

I shook my head. "I have never heard of anything like this."

Maggie had a huge smile on her face. "I may have to see a few games this year."

I glanced at Maggie, noticed her very cute smile and gazed into her eyes. Maggie Ross was a beautiful woman. After being pals for several years I could begin to see that my feelings for her were changing. At that moment, I realized I wanted to be more than just friends with Maggie Ross.

CHAPTER 5

It was Memorial Day weekend, school was out and our team had assembled to play the first game of the year in a tournament in Addison, a suburb just north of Dallas. This was the beginning of our long march to the National Championship Tournament in Phoenix at the beginning of August. Josh Baker arrived yesterday to stay with Joe and me this summer. He had taken the bus in from Lubbock and was eager to play. I briefly reflected on my earlier trip to Lubbock to visit Butch and wondered how the Generals were able to procure Josh's services for the summer baseball season. What sort of deal, if any, had been brokered? Nobody had told me anything and I didn't want to ask.

As I looked around the stadium, I saw fifteen to twenty scouts in the stands. I enjoyed watching games at this field because there was covered seating that provided shade from the hot Texas sun. A red brick, three-story, luxury apartment complex provided a backdrop behind the outfield fences.

Brock Dillard's mother walked past me on the way to her seat and asked, "Lonny, how do you know which people are scouts?"

I nodded toward them. "They're the guys holding the radar guns."

Glancing down to the bottom rows, I noticed three men wearing yellow shirts with purple trim sitting directly behind home plate—it was the LSU coaching staff. The head coach, pitching coach and recruiting coordinator were all there to see Joe pitch. They had sent letters and texted Joe frequently over the last several months. College coaches were not allowed by rule to extend offers until July 1st but they were on the road scouting to prioritize the talent and put together their scholarship allocation plan.

Ten minutes prior to the start of the game the head coach of the Generals, Ronny Espinosa, motioned me to come to the side of the dugout. "Lonny, here's the lineup card. Please walk it over to the official scorekeeper." I glanced at it as I walked to the press box.

Generals Lineup Card		
	Name	Position
	Joe Jones	1
	Murray McClure Jr.	9
	Josh Baker	8

	Mark Heygood	3
	Tyrone Alberts	6
	Juan Francisco	4
	Skylar Huggins	7
	Brock Dillard	2
	Owen Sorensen	5

Now, this lineup made sense! These were the best players and the other less-talented kids would have to wait their turn. After dropping off the lineup card I returned to my seat directly behind home plate in the top row. I had a great view of the field and was high enough up to catch some of the breeze from the south that was blowing out to right field.

We were the home team so the Generals took the field and Joe warmed up on the hill. The first batter on the University Park Gators, our opposition today, settled into the batter's box. The first pitch was a 95-mph fastball on the inside corner that the batter watched. The scouts had their guns up and most smiled when they looked at the reading. The second pitch was a change-up that landed in front of the plate. The batter swung, anticipating a fastball, and was way ahead with his swing. The third pitch was a curveball that started out directly towards the batter's head but dropped into the strike zone. The batter froze and shut his eyes expecting to get hit by the pitch. The next two batters grounded out. It was now time for the Generals to bat.

Joe was first up to bat for the Generals. I loved his plate approach—don't take pitches, if the ball is in the strike zone then hack! The first pitch was a fastball that Joe turned on and slashed into right field. A small piece of sod kicked up into the air as the ball landed fifteen feet in front of the right fielder. Murray McClure Jr. was next up. He was tall and slender but with a good bat and off-the-charts speed. I knew his parents, Murray Sr. and Sofia, well since the boys played on the same baseball team last season.

I would frequently sit near Murray Sr. and Sofia at the games and we would sometimes second-guess the coaching moves as it was so easy to coach from the stands. Sofia was probably the sexiest mom on the team with a mischievous smile. Last year I sometimes caught Sofia gazing at me during the games and I sensed we had a little chemistry between us. Murray Sr. was out of town at a company golf outing today so Sofia was here alone and sat next to me in the back row of the stands. She sat closer to me than usual and smiled. Sofia looked very nice with her shoulder-length brown hair just touching her white top above tan hot pants. Her behavior seemed a bit strange. Then she placed her hand on my leg. I froze and didn't know what to do or say...but I did enjoy it! Was she just flirting with me or hoping for something more?

Then she looked up at me with a sexy smile and said, "You love me." Now I had a much better idea what was on Sofia's mind.

I was not a guy that usually turned down action with a beautiful woman but I was conflicted as I avoided getting involved with married women at all costs and also considered Murray Sr. to be a friend.

But, given the right situation, I realized that I would be powerless to reject her advances. The key for me would be to avoid that "right situation." I looked at Sofia and tried to steer the conversation back to the game. "Murray Jr. looked great in batting practice yesterday."

"Murray has been working with him a lot. They frequently go to the cages after dinner to work on the swing. He should have had a better high school season."

"Wasn't he on the District 9-6A second team?" I asked.

"That's not good enough. He won't get a scholarship to a big-time school at this rate," said Sofia.

Our attention turned back to the field as Murray Jr. was up to bat and lined out to the second baseman on the first pitch. Sofia held her head in her hands and appeared to be in pain. After a few moments she stood up, started muttering something under her breath and walked away.

Josh was up next. You could see the scouts walk down to first base with their stopwatches to try to time his run from home to first. The first two pitches were balls as the pitcher was aware of Josh's statewide reputation for being a power hitter. The third pitch was on the inside corner and you could hear the crack of the bat as the ball sailed towards the outfield fence. It was a majestic shot. The ball appeared to be still rising as it went over the fence. The outfield was surrounded by a complex of luxury apartments and the ball bounced off a large window on the third floor. The window shattered, sending shards of glass down on the sidewalk below. Then a topless woman appeared and looked out of the broken window towards the field. She looked shocked and quickly realized she was exposing herself and pulled her curtains shut. The crowd roared its approval. We were up 2-0!

I looked towards the outfield. There was a lone man wearing sunglasses standing against the fence down the right field line at the side of the parking lot. He frequently glanced from side to side. Mark Heygood was up next. I turned to my right to look at the man at the fence again and realized I knew him. It was Mark's dad, Jack. Jack had come out of hiding to watch his kid play ball. I turned my eyes to watch Mark's plate appearance. Mark fouled the second pitch straight up in the air and the catcher caught it. Then I turned my attention back to Jack and saw that two men had appeared and were slapping him around. One man grabbed Jack from behind and the other was working him over with his fists. There appeared to be a tire iron on the sidewalk behind the man hitting Jack—this altercation had the potential to get much worse. I had Joe's bat bag that contained several spare wooden bats with me so I grabbed one, jumped out of my seat and sprinted to the first base line fence and Jack.

As I emerged from underneath the stadium, Jack and the two assailants disappeared from view as they walked through the parking lot between two rows of cars. I sprinted to the spot and looked between the rows of cars. There was no sign of the three men so I ran fifty feet into the parking lot. They were just ahead of me to the right. I could hear a little bit of their conversation as I closed in.

"Please, please don't hurt me," Jack pleaded as he pushed hard against the larger man's chest. Jack's bulging left forearm bore a small yellow tattoo of the sun.

The smaller of the two thugs responded with a heavy New York accent, "Heygood, you can make this easy or you can make this hard. Just tell me where the money is."

Jack opened his mouth to say something but stopped when he saw me out of the corner of his eye. For a split second I thought about my next move. Should I engage these guys now or run for help? I decided to act and cocked the bat back like a batter in a baseball game. I needed to square-up and get a good swing before they spotted me. I swung the bat as hard as I could but the end of it hit the side of a car in mid-swing with a loud BANG! Eighty percent of my power was lost. The bat continued to move forward and hit the bigger of the two guys squarely in the back with a loud thud. The big man made a guttural sound and grabbed his lower back. Instead of being a disabling blow, my swing had just caused a painful injury.

Both men turned and looked at me with Jack positioned between the two. In an instant they rushed towards me. Jack broke free and left me alone with the two thugs. Immediately, he sprinted towards a car parked in the far corner of the lot. I had not been in a street fight since I lived in East Central Illinois years ago so I tried to quickly gather my thoughts in a few split seconds and plan my next move.

Now that I was within a few feet of them, I realized both men were much larger than me; the "small" guy was probably 6'3" and 250 pounds while the larger one stood at least 6'5" and weighed close to 275. It became immediately apparent to me that I made a mistake intervening in their altercation with

Jack. We were in too close quarters for me to run or swing the bat. Instinctively, I threw a punch that hit the large man in the chest. He winced and kept moving towards me. I turned sideways and assumed a fighter's stance. The large man threw a right hand at my head but I moved to the side to avoid a knockout blow as his knuckles grazed the right side of my face. There was nowhere to dance so I needed to knock out the larger man quickly.

I exchanged several body blows with the large man before both men bull-rushed and got me in the clutch. Shortly, they pinned me against a car and the smaller guy raised the tire iron above my head to part my hair. Just before he swung the tire iron down he told me, "Hey pal, you tried to help that son of a bitch Heygood and he ran to save his ass. Now, you're going to have to take the pipe."

The thug holding the tire iron grimaced and raised it in the air to deliver a devastating blow to my head. I tried to break away from the larger man's grasp but I was exhausted. I summoned all of my strength and then tried to knee him in the groin but my kneecap missed the target and hit his thigh. Then, just at that moment, there was the noise of a car and we looked to my right. The luxury apartment complex security man's car was sixty feet away. He would have a clear view of us in a matter of seconds. The thugs decided to disengage and jogged to their car to escape while I slumped to the pavement.

The security man didn't see me as he drove by and kept on his course. There was little sign of a fight left in the parking lot as the victim and his two assailants had fled the scene. The altercation had barely lasted two minutes. I looked down and saw a tear in my $118 Hawaiian shirt, which was the only casualty of the brawl and now would need to be relegated to the lawn-mowing section of my wardrobe. I got up, dusted myself off and headed back to watch the end of the first inning.

Tyrone Alberts and Juan Francisco had been up next when I left my seat. When I returned to the bleachers Tyrone was on third base and Juan was on first. James Alberts seated three rows in front of my old seat in the last row gave me a funny look as I walked past. "Hey Lonny, what happened to you? Your shirt is torn and there are scratches all over your face. What are you doing with the baseball bat?"

"Jack Heygood was watching the game from the parking lot down the right field line and a couple of guys appeared out of nowhere and started working him over. I grabbed one of Joe's bats and tried to help."

James raised his eyebrows and his mouth gaped. "That was a ballsy move. What happened to Jack?"

"When I got involved, Jack ran and left me to the thugs."

James shook his head. "I never liked that guy; he was always a little bit too smooth."

"I don't know what to think about Jack anymore," I said. "How did Tyrone get to third base?"

"He hit a shot down the line and the right fielder made a lackadaisical throw so Tyrone turned on the jets and stretched it to a double. Francisco bunted him over and the pitcher made a late throw to first base."

I made it up to my seat to see Skylar Huggins strike out on three consecutive pitches. Brock Dillard stepped into the batter's box next and hit a single into the right field gap to plate Tyrone but Juan was thrown out at home plate on a great throw to the center fielder. The inning was over and the Generals were up 3-0.

The Generals continued to play great defense for the remainder of the game. The outfield was stellar and ran down all of the fly balls with the exception of a couple of line drives that got down quickly. Alberts and Francisco were fantastic, smooth-fielding middle infielders that excelled at converting double plays while Sorensen was a serviceable third baseman who played solid defense with an average bat. Completely outclassed athletically, the opposition wore down. We continued to score in the remaining innings, further disheartening them, and the Generals won the game 10-0. The season was off to a great start.

CHAPTER 6

Skylar Huggins' father Jerry was the self-appointed fundraising coordinator for the team. Jerry volunteered to be the organizer of the team's golf tournament fundraiser and also solicited contributions from parents to purchase needed equipment such as a pitching machine and boxes of baseballs. Through these administrative assignments, Jerry had ingratiated himself with the staff and garnered himself a spot as a semi-official member of the Generals organization. Jerry's close relationship with Coaches Randy Espinosa and Stan White continued to grow throughout the season. Jerry was always quick with a joke and fun to be around. I certainly enjoyed visiting with him at the games and would occasionally chew the fat with him on the phone if I had some downtime at work. He was recently divorced and now remarried with a baby boy. Jerry stood a few inches shorter than six feet and had a stocky build with a large head. He wore his blond hair very short and usually had a wide grin on his face.

• • •

I finally finished my last budget meeting at National Airlines and was cruising home in my Mustang GT on State Highway 183 when my cell phone rang. It was Jerry Huggins.

"Hello Lonny, could I stop by your house tonight and pick up your golf team's entrance fee for the fundraiser next week?"

"Jerry, I'm heading east on 183. I'll stop by your warehouse and drop the money off. Does that work?"

"Sure, I'll have a cold beer waiting for you."

I turned south on Loop 12 and headed to the warehouse. Ten minutes later I pulled up in front of the warehouse by the loading dock. "Elegant Furniture & Fine Art" was painted in three-foot high, white letters on the warehouse outside wall. The entrance was open so I started walking through the warehouse.

The batting cage that Jerry had erected for the Generals to use in bad weather was just inside the door. Coach Stan White frequently held batting practice here when we couldn't get on the field. There was office furniture as far as I could see in all directions. Most of the furniture looked out of style: steel desks, lime green, vinyl swivel chairs, molded plastic side chairs, and lots of funny-shaped lamps; the warehouse had the feel of a 1970s business furniture showroom. The finish on the desks and tables looked dull and many of the cloth chairs were frayed. An IBM Selectric typewriter sat on one of the steel desks. There were several large, faded, psychedelic paintings leaning against the wall. One showed a purple spiral coming down from a flying saucer; another had a picture of a woman surrounded by butterflies who bore a slight resemblance to Janis Joplin. The last picture I stopped to look at had a very intense color scheme that seemed to move as I looked at it—almost as if I was hallucinating.

I walked another 50 feet and ran into Jerry in front of his secretary's desk.

"Jerry, here you go," I said as I handed him the check for the golf tournament.

"Thanks for bringing it over. Fundraising for the Generals takes a lot of time."

"How's business?"

Jerry paused for several seconds, took a deep breath, surveyed his warehouse and raised his hands. He looked at me and said, "I deal in high-end office furniture and art. There is a lot of demand now that the economy is starting to recover."

I wondered if Jerry and I were thinking about the same warehouse but decided not to press the point. "Is most of your business here in Dallas?"

Jerry grinned. "Elegant Furniture got too big for Ponca City, Oklahoma ten years ago so I relocated to Dallas."

"Really?"

Jerry continued, "North Texas, Arkansas and Oklahoma are my big markets. I'm going to pull my trailer up to Muskogee and Pine Bluff later this week."

"Do you buy or sell on these trips?"

"Mostly sell but if I see good value I will buy."

I nodded. "That's interesting."

Jerry took a deep breath and waved his hands.

"Well, the business is very lucrative. Some of the people with the baseball team are interested in getting into the action and want to buy an equity stake. They'll get a salary and share in the profits."

Jerry's stories about his business were a little hard to believe so I wanted to move the conversation to a new topic. He was a good conduit of recruiting news and frequently relayed the coaches' thoughts on the players so this was a good opportunity to get some information.

"What's the news on the recruiting front?"

"Ronny told me today that he gets two to three calls per day from scouts asking questions about Josh Baker; he is high on all of their lists."

"That's no surprise. Is there much interest in the other kids?"

"Stanford called about Alberts. Of course, you know, LSU is interested in Joe. The LSU recruiting coordinator asked Stan how big a scholarship they would need to offer."

"What did he say?"

Jerry took a sip of the beer sitting on the corner of his desk. "I think he said Joe would need a fifty percent scholarship."

"What was the response?"

"The recruiting coordinator said they were stretched kind of thin on scholarships and didn't have a lot of money to work with."

I shook my head. "Those partial scholarships are kicking everyone's butt."

"It's nice to know the college coaches respect the opinions of Stan and Ronny; a strong recommendation by them could go a long way in securing a baseball scholarship."

"Jerry, thanks for the update, I need to get home

to fix dinner for Joe. See you at practice," I said just before exiting the warehouse and driving home.

CHAPTER 7

"East Cobb, Georgia is the cradle of select baseball," said Jerry Huggins as we stood in line to board our flight to Atlanta for the annual mid-summer tournament.

"This should be a good test," I added. "Most of the teams in the NCT in Phoenix will be here."

"Definitely the best of the best. Great exposure for the boys, lots of colleges and most of the MLB teams send scouts."

"Is our hotel close to the fields?" I asked.

"The schedule was emailed last night. Most of our games will be in East Cobb, which is a few miles east from the hotel in Marietta." Jerry added, "I think we only play one game downtown at Tech in the initial round of the tournament."

I turned and looked at the long line of passengers behind us waiting to board the National Airlines flight to Atlanta and noticed a familiar figure towards the back. "Jerry, is that Chester

Frizzell in the back of the line?"

Chester Frizzell had an intimidating presence as he stood over 6'3" and had a barrel chest. He was in his early forties but looked much younger as he combed his brown hair straight back and had a youthful smile.

"Yes it is, Chester and Mike are coming to Atlanta with us," said Jerry.

I looked again and saw Mike Frizzell carrying his baseball bag and standing next to Chester. "What do you mean they are coming with us to Atlanta?"

"The staff thought we needed to add an arm for the tournament and Mike is the best one available," said Jerry.

"I can't believe it; Chester Frizzell is insufferable most of the time."

"Look, Lonny, everyone knows Friz is a pain in the ass and tells everyone how great his kid is, but the bottom end of our pitching staff is not ready for prime time."

"The kid is okay but the dad can be very disruptive, I bet he will be standing in the dugout by our second game."

"Ronny and I made an agreement with Friz that Mike will only pitch this year so we will only have to put up with him once a week at the most."

I was a little surprised by Jerry's comment—so he was now involved in the Generals' personnel decision-making process rather than just being a dad handling the team's fundraiser. Chester Frizzell and I had crossed paths in prior select league seasons and there was no love between us.

The flight to Atlanta was a little more than two hours and all of the traveling parents sat together in rows fifteen to twenty. Sofia McClure sat across the aisle from me and was wearing a tight-fitting, red blouse that accentuated her red lipstick. Wendy Heygood was decked out in a sleek black dress and sat between Steve Sorensen and me. Brock Dillard's mother sat next to Coach Ronny Espinosa one row in front of me. The passenger boarding process was just about finished and I fastened my seat belt. Just then I heard a familiar voice and looked up.

"Jones, how are you, buddy?" said Chester Frizzell as he stood in the aisle waiting to get back to his seat behind us.

"Friz, I heard the staff decided to pick up Mike for the Atlanta tournament."

"Ronny and Stan know how good Mike is and thought he would upgrade the pitching staff," said Chester.

"Wait a minute, Friz, our staff is okay. Joe and Josh have pitched well."

"Jerry showed me the pitching stats."

"What—"

"The pitching staff has put up some real pedestrian numbers."

"You don't know what you're talking about."

Chester scrunched up his face, looked down at me and paused before saying, "Lonny, Mike is *The Prodigy....* The way I have it figured, Mike is going to be the ace and Joe and Josh will be pushed down the rotation."

I shook my head in disbelief as Friz continued down the aisle to his seat two rows behind me. Sofia McClure had listened to the brief conversation with Friz and had a grin on her face. I turned to her and said, "I hate that carpet salesman," as Sofia erupted in laughter.

In a few minutes we pushed off of the gate on schedule and took off for Atlanta. Twenty minutes into the flight Sofia McClure glanced over at me and Wendy, saying, "I love these road trips; they give me a chance to play a little. Murray Sr. and I enjoy the time away from each other, it freshens up our marriage."

Wendy leaned her head back and a big smile appeared on her face. "Yeah, I need the break from work and a little excitement spices things up."

Steve Sorensen took a deep breath and studied Wendy's features from head to toe. His eyes did not leave her body for several seconds. Previous summer baseball seasons had their share of parental passion and this season had the same feel. Sometimes parents traveling alone to these out-of-town tournaments paired up, let their inhibitions run wild and fully enjoyed the freedom of being away from their spouses. Other parents sitting in the two rows in front of me read newspapers or worked on their laptops and were completely oblivious to the titillating conversation in row eighteen. If you watch fifty games with people and travel around the country with them, you get to know them. During this and prior seasons, parents would frequently get together after games, especially during out-of-town tournaments, to party and drink. I sometimes joined the group for a beer but was not one of the partying inner-circle that drank late into the night or early into the next morning.

Forty minutes later our flight landed at Hartsfield Airport in Atlanta. Josh, Joe and I picked up our rental car and headed north towards the motel in Marietta.

• • •

Soon after arriving at the motel, I unpacked and took a swim in the pool to relax. After showering, I headed to Joe and Josh's room one floor below me to give Joe some walking-around money. There was no answer when I knocked. I took the elevator down to the first floor and ran into Brock Dillard near the pool. "Where is Joe?" I asked.

"He's in the front lobby with the LSU coaches."

"Wow, that's fantastic!" I said to Brock before I headed to the lobby at full speed.

As I turned the corner I saw Joe huddled with three LSU coaches at a small table in the far corner. My kid was holding court with the LSU staff! There were several glossy brochures on the table and Joe and the coaches were having an animated conversation. The head coach looked like a sales manager at a car dealership as he pointed at pictures in the brochures and looked directly at Joe to make points. The LSU pitching coach gestured with his hands and from a distance it looked like he was demonstrating a pitching grip to Joe. I backed off and let Joe run the show. Joe was going to have his choice of college options and life was good.

I diverted to the motel bar that was straight ahead and saw a contingent of Generals' parents enjoying happy hour. The atmosphere was relaxed as everyone knew each other pretty well. I joined the party and Wendy Heygood arrived a few minutes later. Wendy's son Mark had played baseball with Joe for the last ten years so we had been on many baseball road trips together. She wore shorts and a provocative, almost see-through white blouse that left little to the imagination. I bought her a drink and we talked about our boys and how important this summer was for their baseball careers.

"The boys need to show well in these premier events to secure a baseball scholarship," said Wendy.

"Many of the scouts at this tournament only work the Southeast and probably never get over to Texas," I said.

"Mark would like to go to college in the South so he better do well here," added Wendy.

As we were talking, my eyes would occasionally drift down to Wendy's half-buttoned blouse; I couldn't help myself. She noticed my glances, laughed and winked at me approvingly. Then Joe and Josh walked into the bar and headed straight to our table.

"Dad, Josh and I are ready to eat," said Joe.

"Okay, would you like to eat at the diner in Marietta?"

"Yeah, I heard the food is great."

I turned to Wendy and asked, "Would you and Mark like to join us?"

Wendy shrugged. "Thanks, but Mark wanted to eat a burger at the snack bar and I don't want to leave the party."

Then Steve Sorenson, father of third baseman Owen Sorensen, walked up to the table. "May I join you two?"

Wendy smiled. "Sure, Steve, please sit down, Lonny is just leaving."

I finished up my beer and we jumped into the rental car and headed off to Marietta to eat at the celebrated diner. The diner had a very extensive menu and great food that made the one-hour wait in the parking lot worthwhile.

● ● ●

We proceeded to win our first three games against teams from East Cobb, Chicago and Houston. All of the players were performing well and getting favorable feedback from scouts. Every school in the Big 12 and SEC had multiple scouts in attendance and many colleges in the ACC, Big 10 and PAC 10 were also represented. I ran into Coach Espinosa at breakfast and thought it might be a good opportunity to get a recruiting update.

"Nice to see all of college coaches," I said.

"It feels like a meat market. Every team in the SEC and ACC is here, plus most of the Big 12 and a few teams from the PAC 12," said Ronny.

"Are the Generals generating much interest?"

"Oh yeah, Rice and Oklahoma want Francisco," Coach Ronny continued. "Everyone is in love with Alberts' tools; the Stanford coaches watched our game against Chicago." Coach Ronny paused for a moment and took a big bite of the waffle in front of him, washing it down with some coffee. "I wasn't sure about McClure and Heygood but a few coaches in the Big 12 have called about those guys after their big hits in yesterday's game. A&M wants McClure to take an unofficial visit to College Station on our next off-weekend," added Ronny. "I think everyone will get a ride, maybe not a hundred percent but at least twenty-five to fifty percent of tuition."

Coach Ronny continued to do battle with his waffle and after a few moments looked up at me. "I know LSU likes Joe but I'm not sure how much money they have left. They have offered a lot of players."

"What about Josh?"

"Now that's interesting, the MLB scouts have been on the phone with Stan, me and Mike—he could be a first-round pick next year."

"What about the colleges?" I asked.

Ronny looked around the table, grabbed the syrup and drowned what was left of his waffle. In a few minutes, after finishing his breakfast, Ronny wiped the corner of his mouth with a cloth napkin and turned to look at me. "Well, the big question is whether he can qualify. The grades are below average at best. His SAT scores are even worse than mine from back in the day!" Ronny laughed. "One coach said he would need to call in all his favors with admissions to even get Josh considered."

"So, are the colleges backing away from Josh?"

Ronny lifted his eyebrows and shook his head. "Hell no, everyone is offering and hoping for the best. Josh could carry a team on his back to Omaha," said Ronny.

"Since he is a dual-sport guy, do you think football programs are in the mix too?"

"Yeah, the football coaches usually have more throw weight with admissions so there's probably a back door into most schools."

"So what do you think he's going to do?"

Ronny paused for a few seconds. "He will go with the money and sign after the MLB draft."

● ● ●

After the third game, Assistant Coach Stan White took me aside as we walked to the parking lot. "I know you are a finance guy at National Airlines so I want your opinion on a business decision I plan to make."

"Sure, let's get together tonight and talk over a couple of brews."

• • •

Later that night, we met in the lobby and headed out to the parking lot to drive to a bar and talk. We walked out past the swimming pool and saw Coach Ronny Espinosa frolicking in the pool with Brock Dillard's mother. They were the only people in the pool and were oblivious to everything around them and didn't see us walk by. We looked at each other in disbelief and laughed.

We got into Stan's rental car and headed south on Route 41 towards the Air Force base. Stan noticed the gas tank warning indicator was bright red. "Looks like we need gas now. I'm going to pull into the small gas station with the picnic table on the side of the building coming up on our right."

After Stan finished pumping, we walked into the gas station and saw there was a small hole-in-the-wall Mexican food establishment in the back of the station with one customer standing in front of the order window. We paid for the gas and then walked to the back of the station and checked out the menu that advertised cheap food and ice-cold beer. The tantalizing aroma of the seasoned food being prepared in the grimy, one-man kitchen intrigued us and we decided we would discuss Stan's decision over tacos and cold beer at the picnic table on the side of the gas station.

"These tacos are outstanding, this is probably some of the best gas station food I have ever eaten," I said. "So, Stan, what decision do you need to make?"

"I plan to invest twenty-five thousand in Jerry's business and become a partner. What do you think?"

I paused for a moment, took a drink of my cold beer and said, "I may not fully understand the details around Jerry's operation but, to be candid, I don't see the value of the business. Jerry says his company sells high-end office furniture and art but his warehouse is filled with old office furniture from the '70s."

Stan put the taco down on his paper plate and responded, "Jerry said the company was profitable and this investment opportunity would set me up for life."

I didn't want to sound too negative so I tried to carefully choose my words. "You should do some due diligence before you enter into a business arrangement with Jerry. Have you seen the financials?"

"Jerry showed me a page full of numbers but I only took one business class in junior college so I didn't know what to make of it."

"Stan, I think you should hit the brakes on this one."

"It seems like a good opportunity for me and I like Jerry."

It didn't matter what I said, Stan's mind was made up. After another round of cold beers and chicken fajita tacos smothered with sliced jalapenos, we drove back to the motel, parked and walked by the darkened pool. The pool was closed and the lights were off. We heard moaning and looked over the fence and were surprised to see Coach Ronny Espinosa on top of Brock's mom. Brock's mom's eyes were closed and you could hear her say, "Oh Ronny, oh Ronny, oh, oh," as he moved feverishly on top of her.

We just shook our heads and kept moving.

"Doing a mom in the pool, geez!" I said in disbelief to Coach Stan.

I walked into the motel and proceeded directly to the bank of elevators facing the main lobby. An elevator arrived in a couple of minutes and I boarded along with a couple of players on the Elmira, NY team who were still wearing their dirty uniforms. I hit the fourth-floor button and rode up. When the elevator door opened I started to walk down the hall in the direction of my room. After taking five steps, I noticed a person in the hallway. Wendy Heygood just emerged from Steve Sorensen's room twenty feet down the hall in front of me. Her hair was wild and shirt was mostly unbuttoned. Wendy's jaw dropped as our eyes met. She said nothing. Instead Wendy averted her eyes, turned and walked quickly away in the other direction.

"Wow," I said to myself, "I need to live a little bit!"

I was unsure about the state of Wendy's marriage to Jack but this was certainly a new development. The team's parents made me feel like I was in Peyton Place.

CHAPTER 8

The next day Joe and Josh mentioned there were some room charges so I stopped by the front desk to determine the extent of the damage. Probably the boys purchased a few burgers and drinks. I inquired at the front desk, "What are the charges for room 415?"

The assistant manager responded, "Over two hundred dollars, mostly movies."

"That can't possibly be right." I reached for the detailed bill. "Who could watch a hundred and seventy dollars' worth of movies in three days?"

"Well, it does sound like a lot of money for movies but movie access is closely monitored by a computer," said the assistant manager. "We have never had any problems reported before."

I shook my head in disbelief and handed back the bill.

Just as I was leaving the front desk, Jerry Huggins walked up close to me and whispered in a hushed tone so only I could hear, "Lonny, I have a problem. There's something wrong with my credit card. There must be some misunderstanding." Jerry looked around to see no one else could hear our conversation and continued, "I plan to go to my bank when we return to Dallas and get the problem fixed. Lonny, could you pick up my motel bill? I'll pay you back as soon as we get home."

"Sure, Jerry, you are a friend, no problem. I'm happy to help you out."

"Thanks, Lonny. I appreciate you."

Our next two games in the double-elimination championship bracket were scheduled at Georgia Tech so early that afternoon Josh, Joe and I got in the rental car for the twenty-mile drive down I75 to the Tech campus. Joe was seated up front with me and shook his head as he looked out the window. "This Atlanta traffic is worse than Dallas. Are we going to be late for the game?"

"We should be there in thirty minutes so you won't be late for pregame," I said.

We finally exited the highway and pulled into the Tech campus. "The baseball field is straight ahead," I told them. "I'll drop you guys off and look for a parking space."

Parking was in short supply so after driving around for fifteen minutes I finally decided to park behind a fraternity house and risk getting the rental car towed rather than miss any of the action on the baseball field. The five-block walk back to the stadium took several minutes and I settled into my seat located ten rows behind home plate just as the Generals were finishing their brief infield practice before the game started.

I noticed Mike Frizzell was warming up in the

bullpen and would start against our opponent from Miami. Sure enough, Chester Frizzell was standing at the side of the bullpen giving Mike pitching instructions as Coach Stan White stood quietly in the corner with a frown on his face. We were the home team so Mike would begin the game on the mound. Friz sat down in the first row directly behind the plate as usual so he could closely watch the balls and the strikes. The first batter fouled off the first two pitches but the next four pitches were called balls. Friz frequently shifted positions in his seat, shook his head and waved his hands. Mike's first pitch to the second batter looked like it caught the corner of the plate from my vantage point but the umpire called the pitch a ball. Then I heard Friz yell at the umpire, "C'mon blue, terrible call."

Mike's next pitch was an 89-mph fastball on the inner side of the plate. The batter was ready and turned on the pitch. A crack of the bat sent the ball flying over the right field fence. We were down 0-2. The umpire continued to have a very small strike zone and was not giving Mike any breaks. Friz started to yell at the umpire after each pitch. Finally, the umpire turned to Friz and yelled, "Shut up or get out!"

Coach Ronny held up his hands and gestured to Friz to stop. The situation seemed well on the way to being totally out of control. Two pitches later, after a particularly questionable call, Friz stood up and yelled, "Blue, get off your knees, you're blowin' the game!"

The umpire turned towards Friz, pointed to the exit and shouted, "You're out of here," as he dramatically ejected him from the game.

Friz took two steps towards the exit before

stopping and glaring at the umpire with both of his hands raised—like a man under arrest—for ten long seconds before he walked out of the stands and into the parking lot. Our opponent from Miami scored five runs in the first inning to jump on us early. The Generals were not getting favorable calls on the pitches and they were also making errors on routine plays in the field. Pepe Francisco, Juan's father, was seated in front of me and started waving his arms and muttering in Spanish. Then he turned to me and said, "This is terrible, just terrible effort. Juan is embarrassing himself out there. He is going to blow the scholarship."

I paused for a moment to think about my response as Juan had both fielding and throwing errors in the first inning. "It was a tough first inning for many players. I'm sure Juan and the others will pick it up."

Unfortunately, the Generals continued to play sloppy baseball and Pepe became increasingly frustrated and started yelling in Spanish at his son. The game couldn't end soon enough as we never recovered and eventually lost 10-3.

• • •

Our next game was scheduled to start in three hours so most of the team walked over to the food court in the student center rather than driving to a restaurant and risk losing our parking spots. We picked up sandwiches and sat at one of the middle tables to eat. To avoid the Georgia afternoon heat, most of the Generals stayed inside at the food court after they finished eating. It was almost time to return to the field and the coaches stopped by our table on their way out. Coach Stan looked at Joe and said, "Joe, we planned to save you for the championship game tomorrow but if we don't win this game we're headed back to Dallas. Are you ready to pitch?"

"Yes sir, the arm feels good."

Joe had pitched four innings against the team from Chicago two days earlier so he would be throwing on reduced rest. I wondered if his arm would be fresh and effective.

Our second game at Tech against a hard-hitting team from Rancho Cucamonga, California started on time. Joe was not impressive on the mound—his fastball was only in the high 80s and his slider did not have late break. He got knocked around in the first inning and gave up three runs but rallied to pitch a complete game. The Generals' offense continued to be unproductive and we were held scoreless for the first time this season. To make matters worse, the scouts started bailing out of the bleachers after Joe's first inning on the mound to watch other games. I wondered how Joe's less-than-stellar pitching performance would impact the scouts' perception of him.

After the game, as we were getting into our rental car for the ride back to Marietta, I turned to Joe. "What's up? Why do you appear so unfocused and tired?"

Joe looked down and grimaced. "Josh keeps me up to three a.m. every night watching all of the porno flicks."

I drove off shaking my head in disbelief.

● ● ●

The next morning we limped out of Marietta and headed to the Atlanta airport for the two-hour flight home to Dallas. Since it was Saturday, Maggie volunteered to pick us up at DFW Airport. When our flight landed we headed to baggage claim to get our bags and then out to the curb to look for Maggie's Jeep Cherokee. Maggie jumped out of the car when she saw us and opened the hatchback door so we could load our bags.

I smiled at Maggie and said, "Great to see you and thanks for picking us up," as I briefly put my arm around her waist. It felt very natural and just happened. Maggie glanced up at me, looked into my eyes and smiled back.

"Lonny, I still owe you for saving me two hundred dollars in plumbing expenses."

"No problem. I'm happy to help you out."

We were at the house in twenty minutes and I invited Maggie in for a soft drink as the boys quickly left to go swimming at the Heygoods' pool. We took our drinks from the refrigerator and headed out to the patio. Even though it was summer in Texas, the temperature was cool enough in the early morning to sit outside. We had been outside for ten minutes enjoying each other's company when I heard the patio door start to open and was very surprised to see my ex-wife Joan emerging from the house. She looked at us, laughed and sarcastically said, "Oh my, what do we have here?"

Her unannounced appearance irritated me. "Joan, what do you want? Why are you in my house?"

"Certainly not to see you. Where is Joe? I've looked everywhere in the house."

Joan made a dismissive gesture towards me

with her right hand and took two steps forward.

"He said he was going to Wendy and Jack's place to swim. Next time, call before you come over."

Joan's eyes danced back and forth between Maggie and me. "Ha, we may be going to Europe later this summer, maybe Joe might want to come with us. He could be bored with baseball by now."

Joan knew she was pulling my chain and she enjoyed every minute of it. She moved towards the back door, then stopped and sneered at Maggie. "You know, Maggie, you aren't Lonny's type and besides, Lonny likes younger, full-bodied women."

Maggie's expression fell and then her face became red. I stood up and yelled at Joan, "Let yourself out through the side gate. I don't want you in my house again."

The smile left Joan's face as she took two steps backwards. Without saying another word she quickly walked to the side of the house and was finally gone. Maggie buried her face in her hands and started to shake. After several long moments, she composed herself and stood up. "Lonny, I really need to go now. There are some things I need to do."

"Maggie, I am so sorry. You are a beautiful woman," I said as she turned to leave. I didn't know what else to say. For a few moments I felt some real chemistry between Maggie and me but then Joan showed up and screwed up everything. I hoped I would be able to put our relationship back together.

CHAPTER 9

Things started to unravel quickly for Jerry Huggins after we returned to Texas. The dad who gave Jerry the $1,200 donation for the Jugs pitching machine two months ago went to visit Jerry at his warehouse to find out why the team still didn't have the pitching machine. He walked down the main aisle of the warehouse and into Jerry's office. Jerry looked up from his desk and said, "How are you, buddy? Have a seat."

The dad remained standing directly in front of Jerry's desk and stared at Jerry for a moment. "Jerry, don't bullshit me. Where is the machine? What did you do with my money?"

Jerry was cornered but surprisingly decided to be candid. "I was having financial difficulties and could not pay alimony to my ex-wife so I used your money to pay her."

The dad's face turned red and he clenched his teeth. "Jerry, you bastard, I want my money back."

"Okay, okay, let's give my ex-wife a call now."

Jerry got up from his seat to shut the door and then dialed his ex-wife's number on the speakerphone. She answered the call after three rings. "Hi baby, there is a problem with the money I gave you."

The dad interjected before she could respond. "Listen, the money I gave Jerry was to purchase a pitching machine for the Generals, not a loan to Jerry so he could make his alimony payment to you."

"But I need the money. Can't Jerry pay you back later?"

The blood vessels in the man's face visibly pulsed as he hovered over the speakerphone.

"That's bullshit! I am going to call my bank and cancel the check and then contact the police. Do you want me to get them involved?"

"Please, please, let's give him his money back," Jerry pleaded with his ex. "I will make it up to you baby."

She paused for several seconds and responded, "Okay, okay, I'll return the money. Just don't call the police."

"Make sure I have the money by noon tomorrow or you will be sorry."

Jerry hung up and looked at the dad. "Look, I'm sorry, really sorry. I was in a jam and needed the money."

The man was in no mood for Jerry's excuses. He gave him one last threatening glance before storming out of the warehouse.

● ● ●

In a few days, Coach Stan heard about the

pitching machine story and told me that he had second thoughts about investing his life's savings in the company and wanted his $25,000 back. That afternoon he drove out to the warehouse to confront Jerry.

Stan parked his car by the loading dock and walked up the adjacent steps into the warehouse. Soon he was standing in the doorway to Jerry's office. "Jerry, I heard about your using the pitching machine money to pay alimony to your ex-wife. Why did you need the money if your business is going so well?"

Jerry started backpedaling and soon bumped against his refrigerator in the corner.

Stan took two steps forward and was directly in front of Jerry. "I can't jeopardize my life savings! I want out."

Jerry's left eye started to twitch as he took another step backwards. "Sorry, Stan, I already spent the money to pay some overdue bills."

"You did what?"

"This is only a momentary problem and the company will be back making money soon. You can count on it."

Stan grimaced. "Jerry, you bastard, I want my money and I want it now." He took a step forward and raised his fists in Jerry's face.

"Please, Stan, I'm sorry."

"I want you to feel a little of my pain, Jerry. I am going to kick your ass."

Then Stan and Jerry exchanged swings. Jerry threw a wild left hook that missed Stan's head by six inches. Stan circled to his left and then landed a couple of shots to Jerry's head and chest that knocked him backwards and off of his feet. He fell to his right and his face hit the corner of the desk before he landed on the floor with a thud. Blood gushed from Jerry's face. He scrambled behind his desk and jumped to his feet. His face and shirt were covered in blood. Jerry picked up his desk chair and threw it at Stan as hard as he could. Stan ducked as the chair hit the wall behind Jerry and exploded into pieces. Jerry quickly ran around Stan to get out of his office, leaving a trail of blood, and headed to his F150 in the parking lot. He backed out and fled the scene as a big cloud of dust rose from screeching tires.

● ● ●

All of these developments got back to the parents as they talked in hushed tones in the parking lot before the next game. Later, after the game, the coaches held a meeting with the parents and Coach Ronny announced, "The coaches met earlier and decided that Skylar is no longer on the team. Jerry never paid the team dues to cover coaches' salaries, league fees, tournament entry fees and uniforms. He lied to us for months."

As we walked to our cars, Coach Stan added, "I hired a lawyer to press charges. I want to see Jerry handcuffed and arrested by the police."

This season was beginning to feel like a dumpster fire!

CHAPTER 10

I left work at National Airlines in Fort Worth a little bit earlier than usual to beat the traffic on 183. My head was still throbbing from endless budget meetings and I needed to relax. The Mustang *Bullitt* got up to 80 mph for short stretches between Valley View Lane and MacArthur Boulevard as I weaved through traffic. The windows were down and the blasting radio was barely audible over the gurgling rumble of the engine as I changed speeds. I started to think about my options for the evening. Perhaps I could take Joe out for a good meal after I worked out at the local YMCA.

Once I got home, I quickly changed into shorts and a burnt orange tee shirt. My old, refurbished Schwinn bike stood in the corner of the garage. I coasted down the driveway and started to pedal over to the YMCA. The temperature was cool, an unseasonable ninety-two degrees, so I decided to enjoy the beautiful weather and head north on a bike path rather than go directly to the YMCA. A faint whooshing sound could be heard a quarter mile north of Forest Lane and grew louder the farther north I rode on Rosser Road. The bridge was now directly in front of me. Looking out over the rail, I passed over the fourteen lanes of LBJ freeway. Once Rosser Road ended at the south end of Brookhaven College I did a U-turn and headed south back towards the YMCA. Fifteen minutes later, I pedaled into the YMCA parking lot.

My workout was basically the same routine I followed in high school summer football training in the 1970s—sit-ups, chin-ups, pull-ups, curls, bench press and military press. As always, I stopped to chat with a few of my gym buddies as I moved between workout stations. Conversations usually centered on the troubled UT football situation and the changes that would be needed to make the Longhorns serious contenders on the national scene again.

After a modest 30-minute workout, I rode my bike back to the house to shower. There was no sign of Joe at the house so I thought I would drive over to the Heygoods' home to see if he was there visiting Mark. As I drove, I realized there was a possibility that I could run into Wendy. What would I say to her after our awkward meeting in the hallway of the motel in Marietta? Any conversation could be difficult.

Driving south down Strait Lane about 75 yards from the Heygoods' home I saw a white F150 pull out of the driveway onto Strait Lane and head away from me at a high rate of speed. The truck looked like Jerry's company vehicle but I was not close enough to make a definitive determination. I pulled into the circular driveway and drove around towards the front door. The large, red brick, 8,000-square-foot home had been built by Wendy and Jack over two years ago after Jack's last promotion at Tropical Investments. The grounds were immaculate and beautifully landscaped. The tennis court, swimming pool and guest quarters became visible behind the house as I rounded the driveway. Wendy's brand-new red Porsche was parked just past the front door. I neared the front of the home. The front door was wide open, which looked very strange considering the temperature was over ninety degrees. Something didn't look right so I grabbed a baseball bat out of the back seat of my Mustang GT before I walked inside.

At the front entrance I yelled, "Wendy, are you home?" but no response came.

The spacious living room with a vaulted ceiling was directly in front of me. I walked forward five steps and saw no one so I moved on to the immense kitchen on the other side of the room. A couple of half-filled wine glasses sat on the table near the bar. The room was empty. Finally, after walking down the hall into the family room, I saw Wendy's bloody body on the floor next to the stone fireplace. Her face was badly bruised and bleeding. She was not breathing and there was fresh blood on the fireplace. There was no pulse. Wendy was dead. Someone had given her a rock shampoo.

I picked up my cell phone and quickly dialed 911. The police arrived in ten minutes with their sirens blaring. Detective Vincent Truex walked into the living room and shook his head as he looked at me. "Lonny, I was surprised to see your *Bullitt* in the driveway. Didn't expect to find you at a crime scene."

"I didn't expect to discover a murder when I drove over here. I was just looking for Joe. Wendy Heygood was the mother of one of his friends."

I had known Vince Truex for over twenty years. Vince stood 6'1" and weighed 190 pounds with blackish-gray hair and a dark complexion. He worked out daily and prided himself on being in great physical shape. Since I had known him, Vince had a reputation for being a stylish dresser who frequently took advantage of off-the-rack, two-for-one suit sales at the men's discount store. We had lived in the same sprawling singles apartment complex off of Greenville Avenue when I started working at National Airlines in the mid-1980s. Three rookie Dallas Police officers lived across the hall from me and I partied with them two or three times per week. We were single and just looking for excitement and opportunities to meet girls. The parties hosted at their apartment were legendary and frequently attended by many attractive female residents.

Over ten officers were now in the house. The team of cops took pictures of Wendy's body and started collecting evidence throughout the house. A sergeant took my statement. Twenty minutes later Vince returned to the family room holding the statement I had dictated to the sergeant.

"Okay, so you and Joe know the family. Tell me about your ten-year association with the Heygoods."

We talked for over forty minutes and I described our long relationship with the Heygoods that was largely based on our long involvement in youth baseball. "So, Lonny, you know Mrs. Heygood, you know her friends, and you know her enemies." Then looking at the motionless body on the floor he asked, "Who looks good for this? Just give me a name."

This was a difficult question to answer so I pulled myself together to try to provide a clear response. "Vince, I don't have an easy answer for you. There are many possibilities to consider."

"Well, Lonny, what possibilities are you referring to?"

"Her husband Jack's business swindled investors out of millions of dollars and he has tried to stay out of sight for the last year. I think Wendy was having an affair. Also, I thought I saw Jerry Huggins leaving the scene as I arrived. There are a lot of possibilities."

Vince asked some follow-up questions and requested the telephone numbers of everyone we talked about. I got up to leave and grabbed my baseball bat. Vince gave me a funny look and asked, "What is that baseball bat for? Let me see it."

"Joe leaves bats in my car. I saw the door was open when I parked in the front driveway which didn't look right so I grabbed a bat from the back seat to bring with me to use if I encountered an intruder."

Fortunately, the bat was just out of the box and in mint condition without any dents. Vince decided he wanted to further examine the bat so I handed it to him and turned to walk out of the house. Before I took two steps I heard Vince say, "Do you want to talk tomorrow downtown at headquarters or at your place in the morning?"

"My place at eight."

Vince put his right hand on my shoulder. "Lonny, some caramel-coated donuts would be a nice touch."

I walked out the front door where a small crowd of people had assembled on the street in front of the Heygood home. My window was down as I turned out of the driveway onto Strait Lane. An older man with white hair motioned me to stop and walked up to the window. "What's going on in there? Why are the police here?"

Before I could answer, he turned to his right and watched the fire department ambulance team wheel Wendy's body out of the house on a stretcher. "Oh my God, is that Wendy Heygood?"

I nodded to the old man and proceeded down Strait Lane towards my house. Joe and Josh were just getting out of Joe's car on the street in front of the house as I pulled into the driveway. I walked towards them and we met at the end of the driveway.

"Where is Mark Heygood?" I asked.

"He drove up to Oklahoma City to visit his aunt this morning. What's up?" asked Joe.

"Wendy Heygood was murdered this afternoon at their house; I found her body."

Both boys looked stunned and were speechless for several seconds.

"What? Why would anyone kill her?" asked Josh.

"No idea, but the police are investigating. Vince Truex is over at the house now."

"Does Mark know what happened to his mother?" asked Joe.

"Probably not, I better call his aunt so she can tell him. Wendy gave me her number a couple of years ago when she and Jack went on an out-of-town trip."

Fortunately, I had met Jack Heygood's sister, Sharon Stephens, several years ago at one of Mark's birthday parties so the bad news would not be coming from a complete stranger. I fumbled through my address book and found her number. Sharon picked up on the third ring.

"Hello."

"Hello Sharon, this is Lonny Jones from Dallas. We met several years ago at the Heygoods'."

"Oh yes, I remember you, Lonny; your son is Mark's best friend."

"I'm afraid I have some terrible news for you and Mark—"

"Did something happen to Jack?" Sharon asked, cutting me off.

"No, but please sit down." I paused for a moment. "Wendy was murdered today at their home on Strait Lane."

"Oh no, that's terrible. Why would anyone want to kill Wendy?"

"I am not sure. Could you please talk to Jack and Mark?"

"Mark is here with us in Oklahoma; I haven't heard anything from Jack in six months."

"Sharon, I'm sorry about this terrible news. Please let me know if there is anything I can do for you or Mark."

"Thank you, Lonny," said Sharon as she started to cry and hung up the phone.

CHAPTER 11

Later that night as I sat outside on my patio drinking a cold Coors Banquet and trying to unwind after a very stressful day, I started to think about the likely suspects in Wendy's murder and how everything was related. Then *Whump!* Something flew by me and landed on the table. I jumped out of my seat, fell over and hit the deck. The pale yellow beer can went flying. That damn cat Toots was standing on the table looking down at me on the ground. My ex-wife Joan walked out years ago and left Toots. I think it was her last shot at me or her boyfriend was allergic to cats or maybe both. The cat was very demanding and I had to feed it some Cat's Super Party Mix so it would leave me alone. Toots was a plague on my house!

Finally Toots left and I could try to sort this mystery out and prepare for my meeting with Vince in the morning. Vince was a friend but I knew I had to be at the top of my game when he questioned me.

I tried to concentrate and recount what I knew. The first person that came to mind was Jerry Huggins as I thought I had seen him fleeing the crime scene at a high speed. Jerry was a small-time con man but not a murderer. What would be his motive? I knew Jerry had tried to convince Coach Stan White to invest in his failing company but was unaware of any dealings with Jack and Wendy Heygood. What would be the motive? I couldn't connect any dots.

What about Wendy's lover? I saw her coming out of Steve Sorensen's room late at night in Marietta after I returned from drinks with Coach Stan. I didn't have a lot of details, only circumstantial evidence. Wendy looked very embarrassed in the hallway and we hadn't talked since. Were they having an affair? If so, how long had it lasted and was Jack aware of it?

Wendy's husband Jack or perhaps someone impacted by his racketeering activities at the now-defunct Tropical Investments, Inc., seemed like possibilities. To many investors, Jack was the face of Tropical Investments since he was the person who met with them and convinced them to invest their money into the company. Jack's sales skills were legendary and he could quickly turn one lead into ten. He used to tell me about his frequent trips to the upper east side of New York City to woo investors. Even though he was a practicing Baptist in Dallas he would don a skullcap and frequent the synagogues in search of more investors. Jack had frequently told me that New York was a target-rich environment.

A lot of disgruntled investors lost millions of dollars because of the Ponzi scheme at Tropical Investments. Many of these same people were previously caught up in the well-publicized Mel Weinstein fraud case a few years earlier that bilked investors out of millions of dollars—a double whammy! They would not be happy; they'd want to get their money back and hurt Jack. I remembered seeing Jack get slapped around in the parking lot and my subsequent altercation with the thugs at the Generals' season opener. Perhaps one of the investor's "banking representatives" came to the house looking for Jack, found Wendy and things got out of control? One of the dads had even quipped before a game, "It's good that Jack doesn't attend the games anymore because a couple of shooters out of Jersey might show up in a slow-moving Chevy."

I knew very little about the current state of Jack and Wendy's marriage. Jack and I had coached our boys in a recreational baseball league when they were seven years old so our families spent some time together then but we had very little contact recently. Jack's job responsibilities had grown over the years at Tropical Investments as he became a senior officer and part of a core group of insiders that called the shots. He was constantly on the road going to West Palm Beach, Florida for company meetings or visiting with new investors across the country. At the same time, my responsibilities at National Airlines had grown. I was now directing a medium-sized finance group and also running a large analytics team focused on big data. My job was very high pressure. National Airlines gave me aggressive goals each year that required my team to generate millions of dollars of cost reduction and revenue enhancement ideas. So, our schedules did not leave much time for socializing. Also, Jack and Wendy stopped frequenting the restaurants where we used to run into them during the off-season as they had adopted a much more affluent lifestyle and joined an exclusive country club soon after Jack joined the senior management team at Tropical Investments. After the company's collapse two years ago, Jack was seldom seen in Dallas. Perhaps Jack knew his wife was having an affair, or they were having other problems? I always wondered why Jack was able to avoid prosecution and not end up in prison like the other senior officers from Tropical Investments. I looked through the contacts on my phone to find the number of a friend who was a managing partner of a prestigious downtown law firm. Maybe he could provide some insight. I hit the call button and the phone started to ring.

"Frazier, Smith and Sturdivant, how may I help you?" said the receptionist.

"Is Jim Taggart available?"

"Let me check, whom should I say is calling?"

"Lonny Jones."

She briefly put me on hold.

"Mr. Jones, let me connect you now."

The phone rang and Jim answered.

"Hello Lonny, how are you doing?"

"Counselor, I'm surprised to find you still in the office at this late hour, business must be good."

"As a matter of fact, business has been very good. I had a couple of cases scheduled to go to trial in the next couple of weeks and we reached pre-trial settlements in both cases."

"How were you able to do that?"

"I crafted settlement proposals that made business sense to all of the parties involved. They all got business value and avoided needless litigation expense."

"Outstanding. One question, do you remember our conversation on Tropical Investments, the Florida real estate investment firm that filed for Chapter 11 protection several months ago?"

"Yeah."

"I asked if you had any information on the company and you sent me a link to an investigative report filed with the court."

"Ah yes, our friend Jack Heygood was involved if I remember correctly."

"Yes, Jack was prominently mentioned in the report. Do you have any idea why the prosecutor did not pursue charges against Jack? The evidence was very compelling and all of the other senior guys at Tropical Investments are in prison."

"In my opinion, Jack was probably a rat. Perhaps the prosecutor wanted to send the CEO to prison and needed more evidence to seal the case. Since Jack was the money guy he could probably provide unique insight into Tropical's operation and cash flow."

"So, Jack is going to avoid jail time?"

"Probably so. His attorney was likely able to negotiate immunity in exchange for information and testimony."

"I guess Jack will get off scot-free."

"Well, not exactly. Tropical Investments investors can still sue him and he'll always need to be looking over his shoulder for disgruntled investors and former co-conspirators."

"Yeah."

"The investors were seduced by the allure of guaranteed returns on their investments. They're not going to let Jack Heygood off the hook."

"Counselor, I appreciate your time. Give my best

to the family," I said as the call ended.

That information added yet another dimension to the equation. These were the only possibilities I could think of at the time and was prepared for my meeting tomorrow with Detective Vince Truex in the morning. I set down my Coors and threw a couple of steaks on the grill for the boys.

CHAPTER 12

Detective Vince Truex arrived promptly at 8:00 carrying Joe's baseball bat. We walked into the kitchen where the coffee and donuts were waiting. I poured both of us a cup of black coffee and placed the donut box in the middle of the table. Then we sat down across from each other. Vince sipped his coffee briefly and grabbed a caramel donut.

"Lonny, here is your bat; there were no traces of blood. So tell me, how is Joe doing in baseball this year?"

"Great year so far." I started to recount Joe's numerous successes on the diamond.

"Joe is one of the top high school pitchers in Texas. This past season he was named to the all-state team after posting a 10-0 record. He has great speed and a fantastic bat, and could play at the next level as an outfielder......" After ten minutes, I noticed Vince's eyes were starting to glaze over. Maybe he was no longer a baseball guy.

"Okay, okay," Vince interrupted, reaching over to grab another donut. "Let's talk about the Heygood murder. Tell me everything I should know about Wendy Wang Heygood."

I knocked back the last sip from my mug. "Wendy grew up in Taiwan, I think in Tainan on the southwest coast of the island. She came to the states to study at UT in Austin twenty or so years ago where she met her husband, Jack. I think they were both students in the business school."

Getting up to refresh my coffee, I continued, "Wendy's English was perfect and she spoke with no accent. She sold real estate here in Dallas and focused on upper-end properties in North Dallas and Highland Park. The Betty Hall Real Estate firm frequently advertises in the paper and displays pictures of their top producers and Wendy was always featured as one of the top five in the entire company. She was great at sales—I bet she made over $250,000 per year on commissions, maybe much more."

"How well did you know Wendy?" inquired Vince just before he took a large bite out of his second donut.

"We got to know Jack and Wendy pretty well ten years ago; we were tight for a couple of years."

"We, you mean you and Joan?" asked Truex.

"Yes, Joan and I used to socialize years ago with Wendy and Jack before she left me for her boss."

"I guess your bad marriage was all my fault since I introduced you to Joan at one of the parties back at the apartment."

I laughed. "I often think that."

"But don't forget, when you and Joan got engaged, I told you it was a mistake."

"Yeah, I remember, you said Joan was a great girl to take to Vegas for a weekend but not someone you wanted to take home to Mom."

Vince laughed and took a bite of his caramel donut. "Joan and I dated a few times before I introduced you guys so I knew she had some issues."

"It's for the best that we divorced. I went through a tough time but my life is much better now."

"Are you dating anyone now? "

"I have dated a few women but nothing serious."

"At your last Christmas party, I met your neighbor from down the street."

"Oh, you mean Maggie Ross."

"Yes, the director of accounting at the pizza company," Vince added. "Did you guys ever get together? I thought you two would be a good match."

"We are buddies and see each other frequently. I enjoy her company very much but we are not dating."

"Lonny, she is a prospect. To be honest, I even thought about asking her out when I talked to her at the Christmas party. But I am not going to give you any more advice on your love life. Let's get back to the Heygood murder."

Vince and I refreshed our coffee, grabbed another round of caramel-coated donuts and sat down at the kitchen table to continue our discussion about the murder. "Did you have a falling out with Jack and Wendy Heywood?" asked Detective Truex. "You mentioned that you were close for a few years and then drifted apart. What happened to change that?"

"Jack started to travel more frequently as he moved into the upper levels of leadership at Tropical so there were fewer opportunities to socialize. Also, as Jack's income increased the Heygoods started moving in the upper levels of Dallas society and enjoying the finer things in life."

"Really, very interesting," said Detective Truex.

I nodded. "Both Wendy and Jack purchased expensive cars and built their beautiful home on Strait Lane. I think they felt less comfortable around me. I have a funny story: last year Wendy called and asked for a ride to a game when her Porsche was in the shop. I remember that she snickered as she got in my Mustang *Bullitt* when I picked her up. Ha ha! I think she was ashamed to be seen in my vehicle and didn't take her sunglasses off. Our relationship was totally centered on the boys and summer baseball."

"What kind of a person was Wendy?" asked Detective Truex.

"Wendy was a very confident woman. She always got what she wanted. Wendy and Jack had a weird dynamic in their marriage as they were both Type A individuals—aggressive and dominating. I wonder who ultimately wore the pants in that house."

"Did they argue and fight?" asked Detective Truex.

"I never witnessed any altercations; however, when they got mad they exchanged intense looks and probably settled things later while alone at their house. They didn't air their dirty laundry in public."

"She was having an affair with a Mr....Sorensen, I think you mentioned?" said Detective Truex as he glanced at his notes.

"Well, I think they were having an affair. A week ago on a baseball trip to Atlanta, I saw her exiting Steve Sorensen's room late at night under suspicious circumstances. We never talked after that event and I don't think I would have had the nerve to ask her even if we had talked. I try not to involve myself in other people's business and be judgmental. I don't see a lot of black and white anymore; I see mostly gray now."

"Did Mrs. Heygood see any other men besides Steve Sorensen?"

"Sorensen was the only guy I could possibly link to Wendy."

"The Heygood house was very impressive," said Detective Truex, moving the conversation to a new topic.

"Wendy told me a couple of years ago that they had three and a half million tied up in it."

"I would imagine that the ongoing costs were substantial," Detective Truex speculated.

"I certainly would not want to make those house payments every month and pay an army of gardeners to manicure the grounds."

"I wonder how the Heygoods were able to pay for all of that given Jack left Tropical two years ago and did not appear to have found another job?" asked Detective Truex.

"Wendy's job pays pretty well but probably not enough to cover those expenses. Perhaps they had saved some money during Jack's last few years at Tropical Investments."

"This financial aspect is something that should be investigated—you always need to follow the money," said Detective Truex as he started writing notes in his pad. After a few moments, Detective Truex looked up and took the conversation in a new direction. "So, what do you think about Jerry

Huggins?"

"I thought he was a good-natured guy who was fun to be around, but he showed me a darker side recently. He conned Coach Stan White into becoming a partner and investing his life savings in the furniture company. That was an eye opener. He even tried to stiff me with a seven-hundred-dollar motel bill on one of the baseball trips. The guy has no integrity."

"Tell me about his business," said Detective Truex.

"Jerry buys and sells used office furniture and keeps his inventory in a warehouse off of Loop 12 south of 183."

"Is the business making any money?"

"I would be surprised if it's profitable. I have no confidence in Jerry's business acumen." I laughed and added, "Hell, I wouldn't let Jerry sell my toaster!"

"Ha, ha, I've heard that one before; Lonny, you wouldn't let anyone sell your toaster. Ha, ha." Finally Truex stopped laughing. "Can you think of any possible reason for Jerry to be at the Heygoods' house?"

"It makes no sense to me. Jack is never there and I have no idea what Jerry's relationship was with Wendy Heygood. There are a few parents on the team messing around but I never saw Jerry and Wendy even engage in a conversation beyond a simple greeting."

"You did mention earlier that you saw Wendy leave Steve Sorensen's motel room in Marietta. What was up there?"

"I returned late to my room and saw Wendy exiting Steve's room. She was surprised and embarrassed when she saw me. I assumed it was a one-night stand or possibly an affair."

"What about Sorensen? Maybe he killed Wendy because the affair had gone sour or maybe another reason?"

"Steve is a pretty quiet guy so I didn't spend much time with him at the baseball games. I think he is an engineer in Plano. Have you talked to him yet?"

"No, not yet. I wanted to get some background information first. I plan to talk to him soon. Is Steve married?"

"Yes, Sara is Steve's wife. Sara is a tall, athletic-looking woman who attends most of the games. She doesn't converse with many of the other parents at the baseball games and is hard to figure out. Sara appears to be aloof and usually has a frown on her face. She doesn't seem like a very happy person."

"Any idea why Sara is unhappy? Are Steve and Sara having marital problems?"

"I have no idea if they are having problems since I don't interact with them very much."

"So that leaves Jack Heygood. What's he all about?"

"Our families were close years ago but we drifted apart during the last several years once Jack's travel picked up. So I don't know a lot about his recent life."

"What do you know about his company, Tropical Investments?"

"A couple of years ago, Tropical Investments filed for Chapter 11 and sought protection from the bankruptcy court. Then things started to unravel quickly. The court-appointed trustee soon identified problems with Tropical's financial statements. A former FBI agent was hired by the bankruptcy court to be the examiner and investigate."

"What do you know about the examiner's investigation?" asked Truex.

"Do you remember Jim Taggart, the managing partner of a large law firm downtown who golfed with us at the TPC course a couple of years ago?"

"Sure do. He was a nice guy but he had a really bad slice and couldn't stay on the fairway. I took a hundred off of him."

"He pointed me towards some legal filings and reports that are available on the web."

Detective Truex started to appear very interested and began taking copious notes.

"The former FBI agent who investigated Tropical wrote a 200-page report that outlined the criminal activity. He was able to document the racketeering by a 'cabal of insiders;' Jack was one of six insiders mentioned. Jim called their management tactics a classical Ponzi scheme. The report concluded that the racketeering had begun years before the financial crisis."

"So, did a lot of people get burned?" asked Detective Truex.

"That's an interesting question. I read a few investor lawsuit filings available on the web. Many prominent, upper crust people were mentioned. I had heard their names before."

"Where did you hear their names before? What is the significance?" asked Vince.

"Do you remember the Mel Weinstein fraud case in New York a few years ago? There were many lawsuits by the trustee and investors to claw back money from the Weinstein estate and the few insiders who made money. Many of the same investors were also taken to the cleaners by Jack."

"So many highly placed and influential people were duped and likely have the means to attempt to strike back against Jack and the other insiders at Tropical Investments?"

"Well, they can't get to the other insiders now, only Jack."

"Why is that?" asked Vince.

"The other insiders will be in federal prison for the next five to twenty-five years. Only Jack is still on the loose. He was the only insider not charged in the case by the federal prosecutor."

"Really, there must be a reason," responded Truex.

"I have no idea why the federal prosecutor did not pursue charges against Jack given all of the information cited in the investigative report. Jim Taggart speculated that Jack became a rat and obtained immunity by supplying valuable information to the prosecutor so he was able to obtain the convictions on other Tropical Investments leaders."

"Very interesting, Lonny. Jack and his family could be targets, there is certainly a motive."

"You could be on to something. Jack showed up at the Generals' season opener and was threatened by a couple of thugs. I mistakenly got involved and almost became a casualty before the thugs were scared off by an apartment security man."

"Wow, be careful. Call me if you ever see them again."

Detective Truex stood up from his chair at the kitchen table and headed towards the front door. "Thank you for your time, Lonny, I will stay in touch." Then he paused briefly and added, "Please remember, Lonny, I am the one investigating Wendy Heygood's murder, not you. This investigation is official police business. But please contact me if any relevant information falls into your lap."

"Sure, Vince. Would you like to take the rest of the donuts?"

Vince laughed. "Ahhh, no thanks, I'm trying to watch my weight," and he walked out the front door.

CHAPTER 13

The clock radio came on at 5:30 the next morning but I continued to sleep for another two hours. Finally, I realized I was running late so I quickly shaved, dressed and jumped into the Mustang GT for the short ride to National Airlines. Just as I merged onto State Highway 183 from Spur 482, my phone rang. "Jones," I said.

"Hello Lonny, this is Sharon Stephens, I need your help."

"What can I do for you?" I asked.

"I can't get a hold of Jack, so I talked to Mark about Wendy's funeral on Saturday over at Cardinal Mahony," she said.

"What about the funeral?"

"I asked Mark who should deliver Wendy's eulogy—which of their friends should I ask," she said. "Evidently, Wendy had told him that she found out over the last two years that she didn't have any real friends, just business associates. After Jack's problems at Tropical, nobody gave her the time of day outside of work."

"I'm sorry to hear that, how can I help?"

"Mark wants you to deliver Wendy's eulogy on Saturday."

I was very surprised by this request given my recent history with Jack and Wendy, and needed several seconds to gather my thoughts as I weaved through the westbound traffic on 183.

"Lonny, are you still there?"

"Sharon, I would be honored to deliver Wendy's eulogy."

"Thank you very much. You've taken a great weight off my shoulders."

I began to wonder what I should say at the funeral. I had never given a eulogy before and would have only two short days to prepare.

● ● ●

Clang, Clang, Clang. The church bells rang as we pulled into the parking lot just east of the church. The last two days had passed quickly. I was anxious as I entered the church with Joe and Josh. Inside, Mark, Sharon Stephens and her husband Ray were the only ones sitting in the first pew on the left-hand side. The casket was positioned in front of the altar to Mark's right. As we started walking up the aisle, Mark motioned for us to join them in front. There were probably thirty other people at the funeral, most I had never seen before. Joe sat down immediately to Mark's left followed by Josh and me. The two altar servers were busy helping one of the priests prepare for the funeral. In a few minutes, I turned back to see if I could spot any familiar faces and noticed Detective Truex standing just inside the main entrance. More officers in plainclothes were stationed at the other entrances. I wondered if Vince anticipated that Jack would appear.

The Monsignor and one other priest walked into the church and soon the funeral mass began. "May the father of mercies, the God of all consolation, be with you," said the Monsignor.

"And with your spirit," said the congregation.

"In the waters of Baptism, Wendy died with Christ and rose with him to new life. May she now share with him eternal glory," said the Monsignor.

After the opening prayer and first reading, one of the priests then led the responsorial psalm. Everyone sitting in the front pew was tearing up. Sharon and Mark started to cry.

The second reading was followed by Holy Communion. I tried to gather my thoughts since I would be speaking soon. Since I was one of the first to receive Communion, I knelt for several minutes and reviewed the eulogy in my head.

A few more minutes passed before the Monsignor motioned to me. It was time for the eulogy. I was dizzy. My knees felt like they could give out as I started to walk up to the lectern. Passing in front of the Monsignor, I saw his concerned look. I wobbled up the three steps to the top of the lectern and pulled out the one page of notes from my pocket that I had prepared and placed it in front of me. I looked out at the congregation; Mark Heygood sobbed and his aunt comforted him. I had to focus elsewhere—I was ready to lose it. Vince gave me a nod from the back of the church, which helped to settle me down. As I looked out at the congregation I was surprised to see my ex-wife Joan wearing a black dress and sitting in the back pew. Our eyes briefly met and she smiled. Maybe she didn't mean all of the terrible things she had said about Wendy and Jack?

I took a couple of deep breaths to regain my composure. "I have known Wendy, Mark and Jack for over ten years. Our families became very close...because of the long friendship between Mark and my son, Joe. We have traveled together to baseball tournaments across the country—from California to Florida—to watch our sons play. Wendy supported her son, Mark, through the ups and downs of life...and baseball. I know these last two years have been very difficult for the Heygood family...but Wendy never wavered in her love and support for Mark. She had to raise a teenage boy by herself...which was no easy feat. Wendy was a wonderful mother...who always put family first."

My voice cracked and I stopped to collect myself. After pausing for a few seconds, I continued, "I have considered Wendy to be a good friend who would always bring a smile to your face...because of her sense of humor and wit. Wendy's very successful real-estate career is testimony to her determination to better herself...and her family. She was a loyal supporter of this church...who volunteered to run our annual Casino Night fundraiser two times. Wendy Heygood will be missed by her family and friends."

I folded the sheet of notes and returned it to my pocket and then descended the lectern steps. The mass soon ended and I walked with Mark out of the church behind the casket and the Monsignor towards the black hearse that would take his mother to the cemetery. "Mark, you are always welcome to stay at my house as long as you want," I said.

"Thank you, Mr. Jones, I really appreciate that," Mark responded.

The ride to the cemetery took less than ten minutes with the help of the police motorcycle escort. The casket was unloaded from the hearse and we gathered around the gravesite. The hot Texas sun beat down on us as a few words were spoken by a priest and then Wendy Heygood was laid to rest.

CHAPTER 14

Jerry Huggins and I had some unfinished business as I had picked up his $758 motel bill in Atlanta after he feigned temporary credit card problems and he had not paid me back as promised when we returned to Dallas. I realized that Jerry likely owed many people money and I didn't want to stand in a long line. I drove the Mustang GT over to his warehouse and walked into his office. Jerry's office was a square shaped 20x20-foot room with gray walls. Only a tacky Korean tire company calendar with a picture of a scantily clad young woman adorned the walls. The furniture looked like it was from the 1970s and was well worn. Jerry's large desk occupied the middle of the room with two filing cabinets to the left side. A full-sized refrigerator sat in the far corner.

Jerry saw me walk in and stood up. His eyes were wide open and he looked like a cornered, wild animal. There was a long scar on his face that I had not seen before. I stared at him for a moment. "Jerry, I want my money to cover your Atlanta motel bill."

"Sorry, Lonny, I meant to pay you but my business has slowed down and I just have one nostril above the water. Can you give me a few months to turn this place around?"

"Jerry, I deal in cash; you deal in bullshit. If I don't get my money in thirty days then you are going to have to deal with my attack-dog attorney. He will make your family's life miserable and it will end up costing you a lot more than seven fifty-eight."

Jerry said nothing and stood there slack-jawed. I wasn't sure that he got the message since he didn't respond so I walked over to him, grabbed his face with my left hand and shook it while keeping my right fist cocked. After a minute, I let go of his face and he backed up into the corner of his office near his refrigerator. His eyes were wide open and he remained silent. Then I added, "Jerry, did I see you driving your F150 out of the Heygoods' driveway the day Wendy was murdered?"

Jerry's face turned white and his mouth was wide open but he said nothing. I left his office, walked down the hall to the rear entrance, got into the *Bullitt* and headed to North Dallas at a high rate of speed. The windows were down and the breeze felt refreshing against my face.

• • •

I was driving down Royal Lane and stopped at a red light. I recounted my encounter with Jerry Huggins. Just a few short weeks ago, I considered Jerry to be a friend. What happened? Here I was, burning my hard-earned vacation time at National Airlines to collect money owed to me! Then I heard the church bells ring. I looked around and realized I was in front of Cardinal Mahony Catholic Church and School. The kids were playing on the football field so it must be lunch time. During the tough times a few years ago when my wife walked out, I was sustained by the guidance of the Monsignor at Cardinal Mahony. The past several weeks had been very stressful with the murder of Wendy Heygood and my recent interaction with Jerry. I was beginning to feel out of control and needed to clear my head and calm down. I did a U-turn, pulled into the parking lot and walked into church to attend the noon mass.

CHAPTER 15

The next morning two police cars arrived at Jerry's warehouse and parked at opposite ends. Jerry's F150 was the only vehicle in the parking lot. Detective Truex exited the car at the south end and walked into the warehouse. There was no visible sign of activity but a light was on in Jerry's office. Truex walked down the main aisle and slowly made his way towards the office. Jerry was talking on the phone with his back to the door when Truex knocked. Jerry immediately stood and asked, "What can I do for you?"

"Jerry Huggins, I am Detective Vincent Truex with the Dallas Police Department. I want to ask you some questions."

"Sure, fine, what do you need to know?" asked Jerry as he sat back down behind his desk.

Truex remained standing and started to speak. "You were seen leaving the Heygood estate on the day Wendy Heygood was murdered. What were you doing there?"

"There must be some mistake; I have not been to their house in over a year when I dropped off their son Mark after a baseball practice."

"I have heard many complaints about you recently. Coach Stan White wants us to press charges—he maintains you conned him into investing in your bankrupt company. Lonny Jones told me you lied to him in Atlanta when you asked him to pay your motel bill. I just heard yesterday that you used a parent's contribution to the team for a pitching machine to make an overdue alimony payment."

Jerry appeared agitated and started waving his hands. "Well...maybe some of that is true...but it doesn't mean I was at the Heygood home the day Wendy was murdered. Why would I go to the Heygood home? My son Skylar was kicked off the Generals; I have no reason to ever see any of those people again. Baseball was the only reason those people had anything to do with me."

"Jerry, can anyone vouch for your whereabouts that day?"

"Yes, yes of course. I was at my ex-wife's apartment to see my son. Talk to her and she will tell you the same thing."

"Jerry, I plan to talk to your ex-wife next. I hope she can corroborate your story. Thank you for your time and I will be in touch."

Jerry frowned as Detective Truex walked out of his office towards his car. After a couple of minutes Jerry got up from his chair to see if the police cars were gone. Then he picked up one of the four cell phones in his desk drawer to call his ex-wife. She answered the phone and Jerry started talking.

"Hey baby, just like I told you, the police came to the warehouse to ask if I was at the Heygood house. You know I wasn't there but I have no way to prove it. I need an alibi. I can't provide alimony and child support to you if I'm in prison. You need to tell Detective Truex that I was with you."

"Okay Jerry, I really need the money so I will back you up but you better not be lying."

"Thanks baby," said Jerry as he hung up the phone and breathed a sigh of relief.

CHAPTER 16

The Generals' baseball season would wrap up in another month. Everyone was already focused on the National Championship in Phoenix in early August. The Generals would complete their Dallas select league schedule in the next two weeks. The league action filled in the blanks in the schedule between the elite tournaments. Joe and I were expecting Josh to arrive today and planned to pick him up from the bus terminal when he arrived. I heard a honk in the driveway and went outside to see who it was. There was Josh sitting behind the wheel of a brand-new, red Corvette in the middle of my driveway.

"Josh, nice, very nice, the car is sweet," I said.

"Thanks, Mr. Jones, I got here from Lubbock in four hours," said Josh.

"You must have broken every speed limit!"

Josh laughed. "Most, but not all."

"Is it your car?" I inquired.

"Yes, it's mine."

Josh's answer puzzled me since I had seen Butch's house in Lubbock and the price of a brand-new Corvette was close to fifty percent of the total value.

"How did you get it?"

Josh grinned. "Mr. Jones, I can't tell you that."

I opened the passenger door and got in. Josh showed me all of the car's features and then he popped the hood so I could inspect the big engine. Josh and I were leaning over the engine when Joe and Mark Heygood arrived.

"Wow, Josh, this car is sweet, a six-speed automatic," said Joe as he sat down in the driver's seat.

"What is the horsepower?" asked Mark.

"430, it's got plenty of power; it does zero to sixty in under four seconds," said Josh with a big smile on his face.

"What's the top speed?" asked Joe.

"Well, I am really not sure. I had it up to one-seventy for twenty miles on I20 just outside of Abilene but the road started to get rough so I couldn't push it."

"Let's take this bad boy for a ride. I'm first," said Joe as he glanced over at Mark.

Josh got in the passenger seat and then Joe carefully backed the car down the driveway. The tires squealed as they headed down the block towards the Dallas North Tollway.

Mark came inside to wait his turn to drive the Corvette and watched TV as I started to cook dinner.

● ● ●

Later that evening after Mark had an

opportunity to drive the Corvette, we sat down at the kitchen table to eat hamburgers and potato salad. Mark put his second hamburger down on his plate and looked across the table at Josh.

"Josh, tell us about the Corvette. How did you get it?" asked Mark.

Josh shifted uncomfortably in his chair and didn't say anything at first. "Well, it's kind of strange, Butch's lawyer in Lubbock, Nick Del Monico, gave me the keys to the car two days ago."

"That was nice of Butch to get the car for you," said Joe.

"Not exactly. Nick said he arranged for me to get the car."

"Why would he do that?" asked Mark.

"I'm not really sure. The only thing he said was that I could start on Oklahoma Tech's football and baseball teams next year," said Josh. "Nick played golf at Tech thirty years ago and came to the house with the football coaches to meet me and Butch a couple of months ago."

Joe and Mark exchanged glances. "So, what happens if you don't go to Tech?" asked Mark.

Josh laughed and said, "I might lose my ride."

• • •

We were scheduled to play three games in the next five days but there was time for the team to practice today. Later that afternoon I drove Mark, Joe and Josh to practice at St. Ignatius High School just east of the North Park Mall. It was sunny and over 100 degrees. The turf field was 15 degrees hotter. We looked out and saw the two coaches and Mike Rizzo talking on the field before practice started. Mike Rizzo was the founder and manager of the Generals and a fixture in the Dallas select baseball scene as his teams had won numerous national championships and many former Generals were playing professional baseball. He was a former big-league player and a man of integrity who had become a successful businessman in Dallas after receiving his law degree from Harvard. His involvement in youth baseball was solely motivated by his love for the game.

Mike's business focused on the operational and financial restructuring of distressed companies. As his business flourished and expanded outside of Texas to California, he was not able to spend as much time with the team as he had in previous seasons. But when he was in town he would always lead the practices and coach in the games. Mike now spends the majority of his time in California working out of his ocean-view home in the Pacific Palisades. It was a treat to observe Mike Rizzo direct the team in practice and games when he was in Dallas.

Josh, Mark and Joe set their baseball bags in the dugout and put on their cleats in the grass next to the fence. "Mike is here, so practice should be fun," said Joe.

"There won't be any screwing around today, no grab-ass," said Josh.

At precisely 6:00 the players assembled in front of Mike and took a knee. All eyes were on Mike as he began to address the team. Mike folded his arms and looked directly at all of the players before he began his address. I was too far away to hear exactly what he was saying but Mike's mannerisms and speech reminded me of Bill Wolf, the CEO of National Airlines. This was probably the same way Mike addressed a jury or a corporate board. The baseball players listened intently as he appeared to make several points. After the brief team meeting ended, the players sprinted to their positions on the diamond to begin defensive drills. Mike, Ronny and Stan began simultaneously hitting balls with their fungo bats. The players fired their throws across the infield, hustled and dived for ground balls. Multiple baseballs were in the air at all times so the players had to stay focused.

I turned to Jim Dillard who was sitting two seats to my left. "Nobody wants to disappoint Mike!"

Jim nodded. "You can feel the intensity. More work got done in the first ten minutes of this practice than in an hour of the last practice directed by Stan and Ronny. Mike is a no-nonsense guy, he doesn't put up with any bullshit."

Just then I had a vision of Coach Ronny frolicking poolside with Jim's wife in Marietta. Mike stressed personal codes of conduct at all of the parent and player meetings. Because of his travel schedule he was likely unaware of Head Coach Ronny Espinosa's shenanigans and probably would have terminated Ronny if he had known. Also, it is doubtful he would have agreed to pay the fee to the lawyer in Lubbock to obtain Josh's services for the summer season. I knew all of those sordid details plus a few more but did not want to inform Mike and upset the apple cart as the Generals' marched towards the National Championships in Phoenix. This was not the time to mess with the cha cha!

As I was observing practice, I spotted Steve Sorensen sitting by himself in the stands down the right field line. Should I talk with him? I remembered that Detective Truex had warned me to leave the Wendy Heygood murder investigation to him. But, a guy's gotta to do what a guy's gotta to do. It was time to walk over and have a talk with Sorensen.

"Sorensen, long time, no see! How have you been doing, buddy?"

We exchanged pleasantries and then after a few minutes I cut to the chase.

"Too bad about Wendy, who do you think killed her?" I asked.

Sorensen glanced nervously from side to side. "I was very surprised by her murder but have no idea who killed her, I didn't know her very well."

His disingenuous response did not surprise me given that any possible connection to Wendy or her murder could taint people's perceptions of him but I wasn't going to let him off the hook.

"Sorensen, cut out the bullshit, I saw her leaving your room in Atlanta. How long had you been seeing her?"

His eyes opened wide and his face turned white. Then Sorensen started to plead with me.

"Please, please don't tell anyone. My wife has frequently accused me of cheating but this is the first time. Really, this is the first time. Sara is vengeful and capable of anything!"

"Sorry, Sorensen, I already told Detective Truex of the Dallas Police Department. I am sure he will be contacting you soon."

"Jesus, it was only a one-night stand, not an affair. Wendy came on to me after we had a few drinks at the motel bar. She had on a sexy outfit and said she was lonely since Jack was on the run and never at home. Wendy came to my room later and one thing led to another. I knew it was a mistake and could turn out to be a mess but I couldn't help myself. Wendy always got what she wanted! What if her crazy husband Jack finds out?"

"Sorensen, did you kill her?" I demanded to know.

"No, no, of course not," he said. "Why would I do anything like that? She was a nice person."

Steve Sorensen was a sorry bastard but for some reason I believed him. His wife Sara did not appear to be the kind of woman you would want to mess with. I knew Steve would have a big problem if Sara found out about his dalliance with Wendy Heygood.

I ended my conversation with Steve and moved to another seat ten rows up and closer to home plate to better observe practice. Then I heard the sound of a car pulling up to the stadium and glanced to see who it was. Detective Truex stepped out and headed in my direction.

"Lonny, nice to see you today. Can you point out Steve Sorensen? I want to talk to him."

"Steve's sitting down the right field line by himself," I said as I directed Detective Truex to him.

Detective Truex walked down the aisle towards first base and approached Steve from the rear.

"Hello, Mr. Sorensen. I am Detective Vincent Truex with the Dallas Police Department. I am investigating Wendy Heygood's murder."

Sorensen's head jerked back. He looked at Detective Truex with a dazed expression and started to squirm in his seat.

"Mr. Sorensen, did you know Mrs. Heygood very well?"

"Okay, yes, I suppose Lonny Jones has already told you that he saw Wendy leaving my motel room in Marietta, right?"

"Mr. Jones did mention it, so please tell me about your relationship with Mrs. Heygood," said Truex as he pulled his notepad and pen from the pocket of his sport coat.

"Wendy and I were drinking with some of the other parents in the motel bar late one night after a game. After a couple of hours, the party started to unwind and Wendy asked if she could come up to my room and talk."

"Then what happened?"

"I waited in my room for a few minutes and heard a noise in the hall so I looked out the peephole and saw Wendy knocking on the door of the room directly across the hall from me."

"Do you know who was staying in that room?"

"Yes, it was Lonny Jones' room."

"What happened next?"

"Lonny didn't answer the door; I think he went out for a drink with Coach Stan White. After a few minutes, she walked across the hall to my room and knocked. I opened the door and Wendy walked into the room."

"What happened in your room with Mrs. Heygood?"

"As soon as she was inside she put her arms around me and started kissing me. I told her we needed to stop but she was a determined woman and just laughed. She pushed me down on the couch but remained standing and started unbuttoning her blouse. Wendy was beautiful and I started kissing her breasts. I had lost all control."

"Sounds like this was a very eventful evening for you. Tell me what else happened."

"She guided my head all over her naked body as we laid in the bed. Soon she was on top of me moving up and down. It was pure heaven—the best sex I ever had!"

"Then what, Mr. Sorensen?"

"Wendy quickly put on her clothes and left without saying anything."

"Did your affair with Mrs. Heygood continue after that night?"

"Well to be honest, I couldn't get the vision of her beautiful body out of my mind, so I called her a couple of times but she blew me off. Wendy is a high-class gal that traveled in different social circles than I did. We only got together the one time in Marietta because we got drunk on a baseball trip."

"Do you know if she was seeing other men?" asked Truex.

"I don't know of anyone specific but I did notice that she always checked out the good-looking guys. Wendy was a beautiful woman who could have anyone she wanted."

"Mr. Sorensen, did you kill Mrs. Heygood?"

"No, of course not, I just wanted to get back in bed with her."

The conversation between Detective Truex and Steve lasted twenty minutes. When their conversation concluded, the detective left the baseball field and walked to his car. I wondered if he had already interviewed Sara Sorensen before he spoke with Steve.

CHAPTER 17

The Generals won their first two games in league play this week by a wide margin. Today's game would be the last one this week and against a much better opponent, the Dallas Stallions. Maggie had mentioned that she wanted to see one of Joe's games so I invited her to come with me. I picked her up and we started the twenty-minute drive over to Thomas Jefferson High School.

"Lonny, thanks for inviting me. I'm very interested in meeting some of the parents you've told me about."

"Glad you could come. Did I mention to you that Vince Truex is leading the investigation of Wendy's murder?"

"Yes, I think you did. Vince is your policeman friend from twenty years ago and Joe's godfather, right?"

"Yes, so you do remember him. He said you guys met at my last Christmas party."

"Yeah, how could I forget, he hit on me all night at the party and didn't want to take no for an answer."

"Vince described your conversation a little differently but what you said doesn't surprise me. Once he locks onto a target he doesn't let go."

Maggie grinned. "That's probably the reason he is so good at police work."

I valued Maggie's friendship very much so I was apprehensive about suggesting that we should become more than just friends. I didn't want her to feel uneasy if she didn't want to take our relationship to a new level. There never seemed to be a good time to have this conversation but I decided I couldn't wait any longer.

"Maggie, there is one thing I want to talk to you about."

"What is it?"

I took a couple of deep breaths to try to collect myself. "We have been good friends for a long time now and I think we've grown closer over the last year. I enjoy your company very much when we get together."

"I enjoy our conversations very much too. You've really helped to pick up my spirit since my husband passed."

"I know your husband's death two years ago was devastating so I wanted to give you some space."

"Yes, it was a difficult time and you were a gentleman."

"Thanks, but I guess I want to know if you would like to be more than just buddies. If not, I would still like to be good friends."

Maggie smiled. "Lonny, I've been waiting a long time for you to ask me out."

I shook my head in disbelief, laughed and pulled into the Thomas Jefferson High School parking lot, just south of the baseball field, and parked next to Joe's car. We looked at each other and Maggie put her arms around my neck and kissed me three times. I kissed her several times and then we briefly stopped and looked into each other's eyes for a moment. Soon we were making out like a couple of high school kids in the Mustang *Bullitt*. We seemed to lose all track of time and were oblivious to other people arriving to watch the Generals' game.

Maggie and I were a bit distracted when we arrived at the field just a few minutes before the game started. The field had seen better days—the infield had a number of grassless spots and sections of the outfield turf were brown and crisp from a lack of watering. There appeared to be a large and very active fire-ant pile four feet behind the Generals' dugout. The Stallions could have easily found a better venue to play their home games.

We found seats and sat down. Juan Francisco's family was seated two rows behind us and was well represented with a couple of grandparents, four brothers, one sister and both parents. The Francisco family was a fun bunch and was not offended when I yelled at the umpires so this was a good seat for me. They just laughed whenever I yelled.

"Has Juan committed to a college yet?" I asked.

Pepe Francisco, the father, sported a handlebar mustache and had a big smile on his face whenever I asked that question at every other game. He loved to talk about Juan's future in baseball.

"It's down to either Rice or UT. The old man at Rice is quite the coach. Great school. We liked UT earlier but the coaching change in Austin has thrown everything up in the air."

"Go to UT!" I said, as I flashed the Hook 'em Horns sign.

I had hoped Joe would attract interest from the new UT baseball staff but the only thing Joe had received so far from UT was a glossy brochure in the mail four months ago from the recently terminated baseball staff. No phone calls, no texts, no love from the new coaching staff. I guess Joe needed to finish the season with a flourish and have a great senior year of high school to pique their interest.

The game between the Generals and the Dallas Stallions was set to begin. Jose Ramirez would be on the hill pitching for the Stallions. There were a few familiar scouts in the stands that I had chatted with at earlier games. This would be a great opportunity for Jose to showcase his talents for the scouts against an elite team like the Generals. Jose had put up good numbers in high school ball but the scouts had never seen him compete against top-notch competition.

As the National Anthem was finishing up, I saw Steve Sorensen's car pull into the lot and park. Steve stepped out and walked towards the field. I noticed there were several bandages on his face and both eyes were black.

As Steve walked to his seat, he passed some of the other parents sitting in the first row. The parents exchanged glances and asked, "Steve, what happened to your face? You look like you were mugged. Are you okay?"

Steve stopped and explained, "I fell down the stairs at my home and hit the floor hard with my face. My nose is broken."

Steve turned and started to walk towards

Maggie and me. Our eyes met as Steve passed in front of us and he gave me a dirty look. I wondered if his wife, Sara, might be responsible for his facial injuries. Maggie was not sure what to make of all this and whispered in my ear, "Is that the guy who had a fling with Wendy in Atlanta?" I just nodded.

The Stallions were the home team so we batted first. Jose Ramirez was in a groove and struck out the first three batters on breaking pitches. The scouts had their radar guns out and appeared to be taking detailed notes. Coaches Ronny and Stan conferred as the Generals took the field and glanced at Jose several times as he walked towards the Stallions' dugout. The Stallions were now up to bat and their first batter grounded out into a 4-3 play and the next two struck out. We moved on to the second inning.

James Alberts, Tyrone Alberts' father, arrived and sat down a few feet away from Maggie and me. He was the parent that I most frequently sat with at the baseball games. I was actually in awe of him when we first met as I had watched him play running back for the Jets on Sunday afternoons. James Alberts had put on twenty pounds since his playing days, but still looked very solid and in good shape. He kept a gas grill in the back of his truck and we would sometimes cook burgers in the parking lot after the games. His cheeseburgers were legendary as he usually used two slices of spicy cheese. Joe used to joke when I cooked burgers on the grill at home that he wanted a "James Alberts burger" which meant put two slices of cheese on top of the meat.

James turned to me and said, "I had to take a business call in my car—did I miss anything?"

"Nope, their pitcher is pretty good; he had three Ks in the first inning. Tyrone hasn't batted yet."

"Great. I didn't want to miss his first-plate appearance today."

"James, I would like you to meet my girlfriend Maggie Ross."

I glanced at Maggie and she appeared to be amused by my comment—probably since we had first kissed 15 minutes ago.

"Maggie, very nice to meet you. Are you coming to Phoenix?"

Maggie laughed. "I'm not sure about that yet."

"Phoenix will be a great trip, I hope to see you there," said James.

In a few minutes Maggie got up and headed to the restroom and then James turned to me and said, "Lonny, I am parked next to you. You pulled in two minutes after me. That was quite a display of passion in the parking lot." I didn't know how to respond so I just smiled. James continued, "Are you and Maggie serious?"

"Let's just say we recently started a new phase in our relationship," I said.

We turned and watched the Stallion's pitcher warm up. I asked, "What's up on the recruiting front?"

"Tyrone has received a lot of letters and some coaches are calling."

"Have you guys made any campus visits?"

"Last week I had a business trip to San Francisco and Tyrone came with me. We visited Stanford and talked to the coaches. The Sunken Diamond was pretty impressive."

"What did Tyrone think?"

"He seemed to connect well with the coaching

staff and liked the campus."

"Do you think they will offer?"

"Coach said they would pay fifty percent of Tyrone's expenses with a partial baseball scholarship and thought he might be able to arrange an academic scholarship to cover another twenty-five."

"What about basketball?" I asked.

"That could be his best sport."

"I still remember when Tyrone dunked two basketballs at the same time when the boys were goofing around on a basketball court near the motel and got into a discussion regarding which one of them was the most talented. The competition was over before it started."

James smiled. "The Duke recruiting coordinator called and told Tyrone he was their number-one point guard target."

"So what do you think Tyrone is going to do?"

"I am really not sure and want him to make the decision because he will have to live with it. If it were my decision, he would play football at Alabama. Tyrone said he wanted to commit before Phoenix." James added, "Of course if he is picked high enough in the baseball draft next June then he would probably sign."

Before the start of the second inning James said, "We need to put some pressure on Ramirez to get him out of his groove. We need to play small ball and make the Stallions play defense."

"I agree—Ramirez looks too comfortable on the mound."

The Stallions thought the Generals were going to continue to take big hacks so their infield played on the back of the dirt to begin the second inning.

Tyrone Alberts was the first batter and bunted the first pitch towards third base, reaching first base before the ball was fielded. Then Alberts immediately stole second on the first pitch to Juan Francisco and Jose Ramirez started to lose his cool on the mound. Juan executed another perfect bunt that was bobbled by Jose. Jose turned and fired towards first base but the ball was overthrown and sailed down the right field line. Alberts scored and Juan ended up on third base. Ronny looked over at me and said with a laugh, "I love it when the coaches are on the same page with us."

The Generals continued to score and the Stallions replaced Jose on the mound after the third inning. The rout was on! The Generals won the game 12-2.

Maggie and I waited by the cars as the Generals' finished their post-game meeting. Soon Josh, Mark and Joe started walking towards us in the far corner of the parking lot. Just before they reached us we heard a horn honk and looked to see Jose Ramirez driving slowly by us in a black 1997 Ford pickup truck. The boys flagged Jose down and he stopped the truck. Josh stuck out his hand and said, "Ramirez, you pitched a good game today. That was the best slider I've seen all season."

Jose grinned. "You boys are pretty good too. Tell your coach to keep me in mind if you pick up any arms for the NCT."

"Will do," said Josh.

Ramirez waved as he drove off and took a right turn onto Walnut Hill heading west. Jose was not playing on a good team but he showed everyone that he had the skills to pitch on a bigger stage.

Maggie and I briefly chatted with the boys

before we got into the Mustang for the short ride home. She looked at me for several seconds and then said, "Lonny, this afternoon has been a lot of fun. I finally got to meet some of the parents you have told me about and, most importantly, I got to know you a lot better."

I reached out to briefly touch her hand. "Thank you, Maggie. Hopefully we'll get to spend a lot of time together in the future."

The ride back to Maggie's house took less than ten minutes and I pulled into her driveway. We looked at each other briefly and then I leaned in and kissed her. Maggie smiled and held my right hand in both of her hands. Then she looked up and said, "Lonny, would you like to come in?"

CHAPTER 18

Maggie and I walked into her kitchen arm in arm. As soon as I shut the outside door, Maggie had her arms around my neck and we started kissing passionately. It felt like she was on fire because of the passion in her kisses. I lifted her up so she could sit on the counter as we kissed each other and then I felt her legs wrap around me to draw me close. Maggie leaned back, held my face with her hands and said, "Let's go to the living room."

I sat down on the couch and Maggie quickly joined me. We kissed for several more minutes. In seconds, her hands were all over me as she unbuttoned my shirt. I lifted her top off and unhooked her bra. Maggie smiled and tossed it to the floor. Kneeling on the couch, Maggie looked down at me as she held my face. We continued to kiss for several minutes as I caressed her.

Finally I picked Maggie up and carried her to the bedroom. With one eye, I glanced at the large bed with blue flannel sheets. Then I gently laid her on the bed and took off the rest of my clothes.

• • •

Maggie's clock radio turned on at 6:00 a.m. and 1960s rock and roll music filled the room. I turned over and hugged Maggie's naked body from behind. We cuddled for several minutes and I said, "Thank you, Maggie. You were fantastic."

"Oh Lonny, that felt so good, we need to do this again soon," she said.

I glanced at the clock and it was already 6:30 a.m. Maggie kissed me several times and then I said, "I need to go home and get ready for work."

Maggie was completely nude as she started to walk towards the bathroom and then she turned and said, "Goodbye, Lonny."

I quickly gathered my clothes from the living room floor and dressed. The walk down to my house took less than five minutes and I tried to quietly open the back door to my kitchen. I wondered if Joe noticed that I spent the night out. I took one step into the kitchen and saw Joe sitting at the kitchen table eating cereal. I was busted. Joe looked up and had an ear-to-ear grin on his face. "Top of the morning, Dad," said Joe.

"Hi Joe," was the only greeting I could muster.

I filled the percolator with water and coffee and then plugged it in. The coffee was ready in a few minutes; I poured a cup, grabbed the box of Pop-Tarts on the counter and sat down across from Joe. He still had a grin on his face as he said, "Well?"

"Well what?" I asked.

Joe paused for a moment. "Did you get any?"

My face reddened. I shook my head and then looked at Joe. "Joe, you are a lippy punk."

My son burst out laughing and then continued to eat his cereal and read the sports page.

CHAPTER 19

My cell phone rang as I started to merge into the heavy, stop-and-go, eastbound traffic on State Highway 183 on my way home from National Airlines. The highway looked like a parking lot as far as I could see in both directions. I initially fumbled the phone but managed to pick it up in time. Detective Truex was calling.

"Lonny, I was wondering if you have any new information on Steve and Sara Sorensen."

"Well, I saw Steve at the last Generals' game and he looked like he had been mugged. He has received many facial injuries."

"Sorry to hear that. Sorensen was surprised when I showed up at the practice last night. He admitted to having sex with Mrs. Heygood in Atlanta but said it was a short fling." Vince paused for a few seconds and then asked, "Lonny, were you seeing Wendy Heygood?"

I was very surprised by this question and

wondered what prompted it.

"What? No, I told you before that we were just baseball friends. Why do you ask?"

"Sorensen told me that Wendy went to your room looking for you before she came to his room in Marietta."

I was surprised, to say the least. Had Wendy come to my room to seduce me? She had enjoyed flirting with me in the bar the other night. She was hot. She was flaming hot. I briefly paused and thought about what could have been.

After collecting myself, I had a question for Vince. "Have you interviewed Sara Sorensen?"

"Yes, I spoke with her at length prior to talking to Steve. She wanted to know why she was being interviewed about Wendy Heygood's murder." Truex added, "I asked her if Steve was linked in any way to Wendy. Without any prompting, she asked if they were having an affair."

"You wonder what happened in their relationship for Sara to respond like that," I added.

Truex continued, "Well, I told her that evidence pointed in that direction but I said there was no proof. She did not appear surprised and showed no emotion."

I shook my head and listened for Vince to provide more details about his discussion with Sara.

"She was very hard to read. Maybe Steve had confessed to Sara about his affair with Wendy? Maybe she found out about the affair some other way?" said Detective Truex.

"I think Steve, Wendy and I were the only ones who knew Wendy had been in Steve's room. So that leaves only Steve and Wendy since I didn't tell her."

"Maybe she wasn't surprised by the behavior

because it had happened before," said Detective Truex.

"That seems most probable since Steve was afraid of Sara and Wendy would have nothing to gain by telling her," I added.

"I was unable to turn up any evidence at the Heygood house that would point me in one direction or the other. Steve and Sara both denied that they were involved in Wendy Heygood's murder." Truex paused for a few seconds and then asked, "Lonny, what do you think happened?"

"Perhaps Steve killed Wendy because he was afraid that Sara might find out and the only way out was to kill Wendy. Maybe Sara heard about the affair and confronted Wendy and things turned violent. Possibly, they both killed Wendy as a way to move on from the affair. There is also a chance that they were not involved in the murder and Sara broke Steve's face after she found out about Steve's fling with Wendy."

Then I added, "Vince, what about Jerry Huggins? Have you talked to him?"

"We went to the warehouse to interview Jerry. He denied any involvement in the Heygood murder."

"Well, as you know, I thought I saw his white F150 leave the Heygood residence just before I arrived and found the body."

"Jerry denied that he was at the Heygoods' house." Truex continued, "In fact, he has an alibi that I was able to corroborate."

"Well, I did see the truck from a distance so I guess it could have been someone else."

"We are still looking for Jack Heygood here in Dallas but there is the possibility that he left town," Truex said.

After a pause, Truex continued, "I know he traveled all over the country while he worked for Tropical Investments—maybe he has friends elsewhere who are putting him up?"

"Yeah, it's too bad that you were unable to locate Jack. Perhaps he could have provided some information on the people who were hunting him down."

"There might be a link to Mrs. Heygood's murder but it is a dead end until I can talk to Jack Heygood," said Detective Truex.

There was a long pause in our conversation before Truex added, "Nobody has told me anything to indicate that Jack would have killed his wife. Most of their business associates and friends I spoke to here in Dallas had not seen them as a couple in over a year but they appeared to have a stable marriage before that time. I have asked the chief to send me down to West Palm Beach to see if I can turn something up. The department is under a lot of pressure to solve the Wendy Heygood murder and the chief doesn't want any mud in his file."

"I hope you make the trip," I said. "Maybe do some deep-sea fishing? Give me a full report when you get back in town."

"Lonny, you know I can't do that," Truex said. "This is official police business."

CHAPTER 20

Detective Truex received approval for the trip to West Palm Beach from the Dallas Police Department that afternoon and the following morning was on the 7:15 National Airlines flight to Florida. The two-and-a-half-hour flight went smoothly and landed on time at 11:00 at the airport in West Palm Beach. Truex picked up his rental car and headed to the local police department to check in and speak to the officers who were most familiar with Tropical Investments.

Truex arrived at the West Palm Beach Police Department just before noon. He had an appointment with Lieutenant Rodgers and was directed to his office. Rodgers was sitting at his desk and Detective Truex knocked as he walked in and introduced himself.

"Lieutenant Rodgers, thank you for making the time to see me. I am investigating the murder of Wendy Heygood in Dallas. Her husband Jack used to work at Tropical Investments and I am trying to get a line on him so I can ask a few questions," said Detective Truex.

"Two years ago I briefly helped the FBI with their initial investigation of the racketeering at Tropical Investments. I only met with Jack Heygood on one occasion. As far as I know, no charges were ever brought against Heygood. In fact, I did hear that he provided the federal prosecutor with valuable information that led to other insiders being convicted on all counts and, as a result, no criminal charges will ever be brought against him."

"Do you have any idea how to get ahold of him? I know Heygood spent a considerable amount of time here in West Palm Beach so I have a hunch that he may be living here now," said Truex.

"No, I have no idea where he might be living. You may want to speak with the Tropical Investments Liquidation Trustee, Anthony Selvaggio, who offices with a skeleton staff over at the old Tropical Investments headquarters in the Clayton Towers building."

"I passed that building on the drive from the airport. Thank you for your time."

"Detective, good luck with your investigation. Please keep me apprised of your findings."

Detective Truex walked to his car and started to retrace his route from the airport. Five minutes later he drove up to the front of the Clayton Towers building and could see the Tropical Investments sign on the side. He had no problem finding a parking spot near the front entrance as there were only ten or so cars there and minimal activity inside the building. Most of the offices were dark and the cubicles had been cleaned out. Clayton Towers appeared to have no soul.

The receptionist in the front lobby greeted Detective Truex. "Hello, Tropical Investments is no longer in business, how can I help you?"

Truex responded, "I am Detective Truex with the Dallas Police Department and investigating the murder of the wife of former Tropical Investments executive, Jack Heygood. I would like to speak briefly to Mr. Selvaggio if he is available."

The receptionist made a call and then turned to Truex and said, "Mr. Selvaggio will see you now. Please go to the office in the corner behind me."

Anthony Selvaggio currently occupied the former office of ex-CEO William Clayton. Clayton had been convicted in Federal Court on 33 charges related to the financial shenanigans at Tropical Investments and was now serving a 25-year prison sentence. Selvaggio had worked out of this office for the last two years after his appointment by the bankruptcy court. The office appeared to have the proper amount of furniture but the walls were bare and no personal effects were displayed. Initially, Selvaggio had focused on the investigation of Tropical's finances but was now overseeing the liquidation of the company to provide some compensation to the creditors and investors.

"Detective Truex, how can I be of service to you?" said Selvaggio as they shook hands.

Anthony Selvaggio stood about 5'10" and had a stocky build with blackish-gray hair slicked straight back. He wore a conservative gray suit and appeared to be in his early fifties.

"I understand that you are very familiar with the Tropical Investments leadership team."

"Yes I am; I have been investigating them for

two years."

"Jack Heygood's wife was killed in Dallas. There is no sign of him in Texas and I would like to ask him a few questions that may shed some light on his wife's murder. I believe he is trying to keep a low profile after all of the bad publicity surrounding the trials of the other Tropical officers."

"I participated in the examiner's detailed interview with Jack Heygood soon after the bankruptcy court removed Clayton's leadership team and appointed a trustee to run the company. I have not seen or talked to Heygood since Clayton's trial last year," said Selvaggio.

"Where did Heygood stay in West Palm Beach the last couple of years?"

Anthony Selvaggio grinned. "I heard a rumor that he was shacking up with a former Tropical Investments secretary. I don't remember her name but I think everyone called her Sunny. Nobody ever told me how she got that moniker."

"Who would know how to contact her?"

"You might want to talk to William Clayton's wife, Cindy. She may know. All the other families of Tropical executives have moved out of the Palm Beach area."

"Where does Cindy live?"

"They have a house on Palm Beach Island in a very exclusive neighborhood. I can get you the address."

"Thanks, I plan to visit with her."

"I recently was able to claw back money from former Tropical Investments insiders," Selvaggio added. "The inner circle at Tropical Investments lavished bonuses and other compensation on themselves. Fortunately, we were able to reclaim most of those ill-gotten gains. I recommend you visit with Cindy soon as she will probably have to sell her house."

Truex nodded. "I heard many investors lost their shirts so the claw back will help."

"After selling Tropical Investments' remaining assets, including this building, and clawing back, we will likely be able to pay only fifteen cents on the dollar so there are many unhappy investors."

Detective Truex stuck out his hand and said, "Mr. Selvaggio, thanks for your help, you have given me some solid leads to run down."

Then Truex turned and exited Selvaggio's office. He walked out of Clayton Towers, got into his rental car and headed north on I95 before exiting on Southern Boulevard to head east to the island. The Mar-a-Lago Club was visible beyond the hedges along Florida State Road A1A. The homes on the island were magnificent and Detective Truex slowed his car to better enjoy the sights. The palm-tree-lined streets wound through posh neighborhoods. Soon he found himself directly in front of the Clayton estate. A perimeter wall stood around the property but the front gate was open and a large U-Haul truck was backed into the driveway. Detective Truex parked his car on the side of the street and walked through the gate.

As he walked past the rear of the truck he heard someone say, "Hello, what do you want?"

Truex turned to his left. A striking, well-endowed woman with shoulder-length blond hair stood in the back of the truck. She appeared to be in her early fifties and was probably a trophy wife back in the day. Truex waved and said, "I'm Detective Truex with the Dallas Police Department and looking for Jack Heygood. His wife was murdered in Dallas and I want to ask him some questions."

"I know Jack—he worked with my husband at Tropical Investments before it was shut down. I am Cindy Clayton."

Truex grinned. "You are just the person I'm looking for. Do you have any idea where Jack might be?"

Cindy walked down the ramp from the back of the truck and said, "Jack Heygood was seeing a woman who used to work at Tropical; I think she was a receptionist."

"Was her name Sunny?" Truex asked.

Cindy laughed. "Yes, that's her name. She is sort of a bubbly, free spirit, hippie kind of girl. A lot of the Tropical Investments guys dug her."

"What was Heygood's relationship with her?"

"I think Sunny slept with half of the management guys at the company before she dated Jack. Once that relationship started she was more discreet with her other flings." Cindy laughed and continued, "But I know she helped several middle-aged men make it through their mid-life crises."

Truex smiled at Cindy and said, "When did Sunny's affair with Jack begin?"

"I started to see them together socially about three years ago, one year before Tropical Investments filed for Chapter 11. They didn't try to hide their relationship here in Palm Beach."

"Really?"

"Sunny must have thought Jack would be a good meal ticket and Jack wanted something different than Wendy—his very intense wife. All of the guys, including my husband Bill, said Sunny was wild in bed. Jack made a lot of trips down here and they were not all for business."

"Do you have any idea where I might find Sunny?"

"A couple of months ago I ran into an accountant who used to work at Tropical Investments and he said Sunny works as a waitress in a bar that he frequents on Federal Highway in Delray Beach."

"Is Delray Beach close?"

"It's the next town south of Boynton Beach."

"Do you remember the name of the bar?"

"I think it's The Beachcomber."

"Thank you, Mrs. Clayton," said Detective Truex before he walked back to his car. It was now 3:00 and the bar would be open so Truex did a U-turn and headed south of town to look for Sunny.

Detective Truex made his way in heavy traffic to the south side of Delray Beach and spotted a sign for The Beachcomber. He pulled into the lot where ten cars and several motorcycles were parked.

Truex walked in and sat at the large circular bar. There were several large fish mounted on the wall and the interior had a tropical feel. A young waitress wearing hot pants and a halter top was talking to two businessmen on the opposite side of the bar. She had bleached-blond hair and a curvaceous body. Truex noticed a large bright yellow tattoo on her shoulder. From a distance it looked a sun with a smiling face in the middle. The waitress turned, looked at Truex and welcomed him to the bar.

"Hi there, what would you like to drink?"

"I am looking for a woman named Sunny that works at this bar."

The waitress smiled. "That would be me, honey."

"Okay, now I get it." Detective Truex laughed.

"Your nickname and the tattoo."

"Everyone gets Sunny," she said as she winked at him.

Detective Truex had a very businesslike demeanor but his face turned bright red after Sunny's forward comment. He was able to quickly regain his composure and started to ask some questions.

"I am Detective Vincent Truex with the Dallas Police Department and am looking for Jack Heygood. Do you know where I might find him?"

The smile quickly left Sunny's face and her eyes opened wide. "My name is Angelica Austin; Jack and I are friends but I have not seen him in a couple of months."

"Where did Jack say he was going before he left?"

"I think he said he was going to Dallas to see his son play baseball and get some money."

"Does Jack stay with you when he comes to Palm Beach?"

"Jack frequently stays with me in our studio apartment across the street."

"Here's my business card. Please tell Jack that he needs to contact me as soon as possible. Thank you for your time."

Obtaining a search warrant to the apartment that Jack and Sunny shared would be very difficult in South Florida because Detective Truex couldn't link Jack to a crime and he was not on his home turf of Dallas. Truex parked his car in a position at the east side of the lot that provided a clear view of the apartment complex and the door to Sunny's apartment. There was no sign of activity in the apartment and all of the lights were out. Detective

Truex hunkered down in his car and waited.

Several hours passed and the sun set. Later, around midnight, Truex looked up to see three men walking through the apartment complex parking lot. When the men were within thirty feet of Truex's car they noticed the front window was open on the driver's side. They stopped and walked towards the car.

Finally they saw Detective Truex sitting low in the front seat. One of the men said to Truex, "Hey man, what are you doing in the car? Are you some kind of pervert?"

The men laughed for a few seconds but Detective Truex remained silent. The smaller of the guys wearing a baseball hat took a couple of steps towards him and said, "You have any money?"

Detective Truex did not respond and the man took another couple steps forward. He was now within five feet of the car. "It's a rental car," the man said as he turned to the two men standing behind him. "Let's take the rental for a ride," said the man turning towards Detective Truex. "Why don't you get out of the car and toss me the keys, we won't hurt you."

They waited for Truex to respond but he said nothing. "Well, what's it going to be?" said the man with the baseball hat as he took a couple of steps forward and raised his hands. The Glock 27 pistol with hollow point bullets had been in Truex's hand for the last five minutes. This was the backup pistol he used on the job in Dallas and was easy to conceal. He raised the gun and pointed it at the men.

"If you boys blow my stakeout I am going to shoot you where you stand," said Detective Truex. The men froze and their eyes opened wide. They looked at each other and sprinted in the other direction as fast as they could. Truex shook his head and looked around for any sign of activity but saw nothing.

About 2:30 a.m. Truex spotted Sunny and one of the customers he had seen earlier in The Beachcomber holding hands and walking across the street towards the apartment. They walked up the stairs to her second-floor apartment. Sunny looked in her purse to grab the key but fumbled it as the customer stood behind her and fondled her breasts. They laughed and kissed. Soon they were inside and turned on the lights. The lights went off around 3:00 and there was no sign of activity at the apartment until 11:00 when Sunny and the customer walked out of the apartment arm in arm. After witnessing these developments and with no sign of Jack, Detective Truex drove back towards the rental car facility at the airport to return his car and fly back to Dallas.

CHAPTER 21

I had just finished my third budget meeting of the day and was finally alone in my office at National Airlines. I glanced out of my fourth-floor window west towards State Highway 360. Southbound traffic had stopped; it looked like a parking lot. I shook my head. Then the phone rang. "Jones," I announced.

"Hi buddy, how are you doing?" said the familiar voice. It was Jerry Huggins.

"Huggins, do you have my money?"

"As a matter of fact, I have it all in an envelope in my office. I had to jump through firelit hoops to get it!"

"Don't pat yourself on the back."

"C'mon Lonny, why don't you come by the warehouse today to pick it up and drink a couple of beers with me?"

I quickly checked my calendar and there were no other meetings scheduled for today.

"I'm on my way," I said as I hung up the phone

and started walking out to the parking garage. I merged onto eastbound 183 towards Dallas; it would be a short ride in the Mustang GT to Jerry's warehouse off of Loop 12. Traffic was surprisingly light so I made good time even though there was extensive road construction in process to add multiple lanes in both directions. Once I arrived at Jerry's warehouse, I parked in back and walked down the main hallway. Jerry was talking with his secretary at her desk outside of his office. I was in front of them in thirty seconds.

"Okay Jerry, let me see my money."

Jerry nodded and we walked into his office where he removed a thick envelope from a locked filing cabinet to the left of his desk.

"Here you go. Can I get you a beer?" said Jerry as he handed me the envelope.

I counted the money, it was all there. There were still many unanswered questions about the reason for Jerry's visit to the Heygoods' house on the day Wendy was murdered, so why not ask him now?

"So, let me ask you a question, Jerry—what were you doing at the Heygoods' house the day Wendy was killed? Detective Truex said you have an alibi but I am not buying it. I know you were there, I just don't know why."

Jerry looked at me for a moment, paused and then responded, "I was trying to find Jack and went to the house to look for him. Wendy was lying on the floor dead when I arrived. So I got out of there as quickly as possible."

"Why were you looking for Jack?"

"He and I had some prior business dealings and I thought he could loan me some money," said Jerry.

"What possible business relationship could you

have with Jack? He was into multi-million-dollar real estate investments while you deal in old office furniture. That doesn't make any sense."

Jerry laughed, opened a beer, sat down at his desk and then propped his feet on top of it.

"A few years ago before Tropical Investments went belly-up, Jack started skimming money from some of their accounts. He thought the money could be hot—maybe the Feds were tracing it? So he approached me about using my furniture company to launder the money. I would exchange his money for a small transaction fee."

"How did it work?"

"If Jack came over here with a suitcase with a hundred thousand of dirty money he would leave with eighty thousand clean."

Jerry took a couple of sips from his beer. "I buy and sell office furniture in towns all over this part of the country and all of my transactions are in cash."

"How long did this arrangement last?"

"We worked together for three years but it all stopped two years ago when Tropical Investments was taken over by the bankruptcy court. I probably laundered over a million dollars for Jack."

"So you were running a scam within a scam—running a bogus furniture business that bilked your small-time investors while also laundering money for Jack."

A big smile appeared on Jerry's face. He was proud of himself and showed absolutely no remorse. "Yeah, I was making some money doing all of that plus I had a couple of other games on the side. Lonny, if you tell Truex any of this I will deny that this conversation took place."

Jerry had no shame.

I laughed and said, "Jerry, you are a son of a bitch!" as I grabbed a cold beer from the refrigerator in the far corner and walked out of his office towards the parking lot.

"Lonny, good luck in Phoenix. Let's go out for a beer sometime after you get back in town," I heard him yell behind me.

Jerry was a horse's ass, but deep down, I still liked him a little bit. You had to admire his *chutzpah*!

CHAPTER 22

The trip to Phoenix was less than two weeks away. We had our tickets and already started to pack. Josh was supposed to arrive this morning but we had not heard from him. The phone rang and I picked it up.

"Hi Mr. Jones, this is Josh and I'm at the bus station, can someone pick me up?"

"Sure Josh, I think Joe is at a movie with his girlfriend so I will get you. See you in thirty minutes."

I got in the Mustang GT and blasted south down the Dallas North Tollway towards downtown Dallas. Traffic was light as it was a Sunday afternoon so I was able to reach 90 mph between Northwest Highway and Mockingbird. I pulled into the bus station parking lot and Josh emerged carrying his baseball bag and a suitcase.

"Hi Josh, nice to see you."

"Thanks, Mr. Jones, for coming downtown to pick me up."

"Josh, I guess I am a little surprised, I thought you would drive your Corvette from Lubbock to Dallas."

"I don't have the car anymore."

"What?"

"A few weeks ago, the football coaches from one of the top teams in the country started to call and then they flew out to Lubbock to talk to me."

Josh paused so I asked, "What happened?"

"They asked me to run some unofficial forty-yard dashes for them over on the high school football field to check my speed. I ran times of 4.4 and 4.45 seconds and they immediately offered me a full-ride football scholarship," said Josh.

"Wow, that was an illegal workout," I said.

Josh looked out the window and said, "I had committed to Oklahoma Tech a month ago but this new offer changed everything. Tech is a program on the rise trying to get better while that school has been in the college football playoffs each of the last two years."

Suddenly a sea of red lights appeared in front of us and the traffic slowed. The red firetruck blocked the right lane and everyone tried to merge left. Two badly damaged cars were parked to the side of the tollway. Joe viewed the scene and continued, "The school immediately flew me out to Los Angeles on a recruiting trip. The private jet was sweet! It was a great trip—I saw the ocean and went surfing; also, I met some really nice coeds."

Josh glanced out of the window as we passed Northwest Highway going north on the Dallas North Tollway and continued, "Well, Butch's lawyer heard about the coaches' visit and my trip to Los Angeles. He called me to his office and said I was a worthless son of a bitch that would end up like Butch. Then he took the keys to the Corvette and told me I could walk or take a bus! So here I am. The ride from Lubbock on 'The Dog' wasn't that bad," said Josh, with a big smile on his face.

You had to admire Josh for choosing his own direction as it would have been very tempting to keep his prior commitment to Oklahoma Tech and the red Corvette. We exited at Walnut Hill and headed directly to my house. As we pulled up we saw Joe and Mark Heygood shooting hoops in the driveway. They stopped and glanced at my car. Both had puzzled looks on their faces when they saw Josh. He got out of my car, threw up his hands and told them, "It's a long story."

As the boys started to talk, Detective Truex drove up and parked on the street. He quickly got out of his car and walked over to Joe. "How is my godson doing?" said Vince.

"Vince, nice to see you," said Joe.

Vince reached into his wallet, grabbed a twenty-dollar bill and handed it to Joe.

"Thanks, Vince. I can use the money." Joe smiled.

Detective Truex turned and walked towards me.

"Hey Vince, *cómo está?*" I said.

"*Bien, bien,*" answered Vince. He looked like he wanted to talk.

"Vince, let's step inside and let these boys play ball."

We walked into the living room and sat down.

"How was that boondoggle in Florida? Catch many fish?" I asked.

"No, unfortunately the trip was short and all business."

"Did you locate Jack?"

"No, but I found out he has been playing house with this hot, hippie waitress for the last few years. She used to work with Jack at Tropical Investments."

"Wow! Really, maybe Wendy and Jack had an open marriage?"

Vince grinned. "They certainly didn't seem to be respecting their vows."

There was a moment of silence. Vince looked at me for a moment and said, "There may be a bigger financial angle to this case than I ever considered before."

"What's that?" I asked.

"The Tropical Investments Liquidation Trustee said he was able to claw back much of the ill-gotten gains from the Tropical Investments senior leadership team. The claw back and the legal fees Jack paid his defense lawyers to represent him and negotiate his deal to avoid prosecution should have exhausted most of his funds."

"That's good," I said. "So what's the new financial angle on your case?"

"Jack must have access to plenty of money; he's still making large house payments each month here in Dallas and living a double life in Florida. Something is not adding up." Vince paused for a moment, his brow furrowed. "Maybe there is something the bankruptcy court examiner and the FBI did not turn up in their investigations of Tropical Investments."

"I bet those two thugs who tried to get money from Jack in the parking lot at the season opener must have known something. If they were just sent to inflict pain on Jack to revenge the Ponzi scheme then they could have easily done that," I said.

"Are you aware of any other possible sources of income for Jack Heygood?" asked Detective Truex.

"Well, I did hear something interesting. Jerry Huggins came up with the seven fifty-eight he owed me from the Atlanta trip and invited me to his warehouse to get it."

"What did he say?" asked Truex.

"He told me he laundered money for Jack."

"Really?"

"He will deny it if you confront him and it would be hard to prove since all of Jerry's business transactions are in cash. Jerry is a serial liar so I didn't put much stock in his story."

"Maybe that story is true but you wonder how Jerry got his hands on the money as it must have been outside of Jack's Tropical Investments compensation package that the investigators were aware of and clawed back," said Detective Truex.

We heard a knock at the front door and turned to see Maggie Ross walk in. She looked particularly stunning in her white blouse and light tan shorts. Both Vince and I noticed and our eyes widened.

"Maggie, do you remember Vince Truex from my Christmas party?"

Maggie had a mischievous smile on her face. "Hi Vince. I never forget a guy who hits on me at a Christmas party."

Vince blushed but appreciated the friendly jab and laughed as a big smile appeared on his face. "You do know that I have been telling Lonny to ask you out for the last several months?" retorted Vince.

Maggie just shook her head. "You guys looked pretty serious when I saw you through the window; I bet you are talking about the Heygood murder case?"

"Yes, we can't explain how Jack Heygood would still have enough money to cover his expenses here in Dallas and in Florida," said Vince.

After a brief pause, Vince continued, "We think there is a possibility he was stealing from Tropical Investments. Maybe his co-conspirators in the Ponzi scheme were not even aware of it."

"Besides, Jerry told me he was laundering money for Jack but you never know when he is telling a lie." I added, "Maggie, you are a director of accounting and a CPA, what do you think?"

"Well, I have only read the first two pages of the examiner's report but I will let you know once I finish. I had to investigate several cases of fraud when I worked for a Big Four accounting firm and audited companies," said Maggie.

"Please let me know if you come up with any ideas because we may have to chase the money to solve Wendy Heygood's murder," Vince told her.

Detective Truex waved as he walked back outside. Maggie and I saw him talk to the boys who were playing basketball in the driveway for a few minutes before he drove away.

Maggie and I were finally alone in the house. "Would you care for a Diet Coke?" I asked.

"Sure, that would be great," Maggie said as we turned and walked into the kitchen.

I got a couple of cans out of the refrigerator and we sat down next to each other at the kitchen table. We gazed at each other for several minutes and then Maggie held my hand. "I need to tell you about the news at work," said Maggie.

"What's it about?" I asked.

"My boss, the District VP based in Houston, turned in his resignation yesterday. He was burned out and wanted to spend more time with his teenage kids. The kids were doing some crazy stuff and he couldn't be an effective parent working fifty to sixty hours every week."

"How will that impact you?"

"Well, the company has asked me to fill in for him on a temporary basis."

"That could be a great opportunity."

"Yes, I think so, but I will need to temporarily relocate to Houston."

This was not good news for me but I smiled and tried to remain positive.

"How long will you be in Houston?" I asked.

"I have to fly down in a couple of days and should be back by the second week of August, just before you guys go to the NCT in Phoenix." Maggie smiled broadly and added, "This will be a nice opportunity to visit with girls."

I studied Maggie's face. "The office is on the west side of Houston, right?"

"Yes, on Memorial, a couple of miles from Mary's house."

"Since she is pregnant, I'm sure she will appreciate the support and the help to prepare for the baby."

"Yes, I can hardly wait. Mary's house has a couple of extra bedrooms so I will stay with them."

I had briefly thought that I might fly down to Houston and spend a romantic weekend with Maggie at her hotel but this development put a kibosh on that idea.

"Well, I need to start packing for Houston so I need to run," said Maggie as she got up to leave.

Even though Maggie was going to be gone a short time I was not happy and knew I was going to miss her.

I was starting to wash the dirty dishes in the sink when I heard the back door open and Mark Heygood walked inside. Mark sat down at the kitchen table and said, "Mr. Jones, do you know what happened to my dad?"

I dried my hands off and sat down with Mark at the table. "I don't know where he is. Detective Truex flew down to Florida to talk with him but couldn't find him." I paused for a moment and continued, "Some people Detective Truex talked with in West Palm Beach think your dad is spending time in that area but we don't know for sure."

Mark looked around and shook his head. "I know he likes Florida. Last year, he asked me if I wanted to move down there with him."

"Really? What did you tell him?"

Tears started to run down Mark's face. He said, "I told him I wanted to stay with Mom in Dallas."

"I am very sorry to hear that."

"We never really talked much after that," said Mark with a sigh.

There was a moment of silence as we looked at each other. I could feel his pain. Then there was a sound to my right and we both turned. The door swung open and Josh walked into the kitchen holding a basketball. "C'mon Heygood, get your butt out there on the driveway. I am going to school you in hoops."

The conversation was over as both boys quickly left the kitchen. I felt relieved that the conversation was over since I didn't want to burden Mark with the sordid details I had discovered of Jack's life.

CHAPTER 23

The next afternoon Mark Heygood walked out on the back patio as I was sweeping up. "Mr. Jones, I spoke to my aunt Sharon today. She is going to be staying in Dallas for a couple of weeks at my house."

Mark had a very serious expression on his face so I set down the broom and dustpan and motioned for him to sit at the table. I wanted to be completely focused on our conversation. We sat next to each other near the grass, facing the house.

"That's great, I'm sure she will be glad to see you."

"So, I'll be able to move home for a while," said Mark. "She said the house is on sale for three point seven million and will probably sell quickly."

"It is priced to sell. Somebody is going to get a good deal," I said.

"After we get back from the NCT, I'm moving up to Oklahoma City to live with my aunt for my senior of high school." Mark continued, "She said I was admitted to a prep school there."

"Maybe next summer you can stay with Joe and me and play on the Generals."

"Mr. Rizzo told me last week that he wanted me to play for him next summer."

I looked at Mark and smiled. "That's great news. Joe and I would love to have you back."

Mark looked at me for several seconds and the smile left his face. "One other thing, thanks for listening to me talk about my parents; this has been very hard for me."

"Any time you want to talk with someone this summer or next year, give me a call," I said as I patted Mark on the back.

"Thanks, Mr. Jones," said Mark just before he stood and walked into the house.

Several players on the Generals had been offered baseball scholarships and had committed to schools. I got the scoop when I sat down for dinner with Joe, Josh and Mark that evening.

"I was really surprised to hear that Alberts decided to play baseball at Stanford," said Joe.

Josh chimed in, "Yeah, he seemed like a lock to play basketball at Duke earlier in the summer. Glad to hear TCU offered Sorenson; he was excited to be able to play close to home."

"Francisco wanted to go to Rice but the old man pulled the offer a couple of weeks ago. There was talk that he didn't make it through admissions," Mark added. "He was talking up the University of Houston at our last practice."

"Joe, where do you think you will end up?" asked Josh.

"Initially, LSU seemed like a done deal but after the last game I pitched in Atlanta, I don't feel the same love from the staff. I think I am on their backup list. If one of their recruiting targets decides to go elsewhere then they might offer," said Joe.

"What about UT?" asked Mark.

Joe leaned back in his chair, tilted his head sideways and raised his hands. "I sure wish the new UT staff would show some interest. When I contacted them earlier, they recommended I attend one of their baseball camps so they could take a look at me," said Joe.

"Josh, are you going to play in LA?" asked Mark.

"Well, the football scholarship is a one-hundred-percent ride," Josh said. "Everything will be paid for which sure beats a partial baseball scholarship."

"What does your dad think?" Joe asked.

"I visited Butch in jail last week and he said he might want to get more involved in my decision at some point so you never know what that means. He also told me he might be able to make bail next week before he goes on trial in September."

• • •

I wanted to spend time with Maggie before she left for Houston, so after washing the dinner dishes, I walked over to Maggie's house and found her poring through documents on her computer. All three of her monitors displayed information about Tropical Investments.

"Maggie, you look serious. Am I interrupting your work?"

"No, no, I read the examiner's report on Tropical Investments and found several other interesting documents online."

"Do you have any idea how Jack was able to get

his hands on a lot of money without anyone knowing it?" I asked.

"Here's what I discovered; Tropical Investments started laying off people working at their headquarters several years before the Ponzi scheme was exposed. They probably did this to reduce their expenses since they were not making any money," said Maggie.

"What does that have to do with Jack?"

"Jack was Senior Vice President of Marketing and also a CPA. When the large layoffs occurred in the accounting department and the controller left, Jack filled in as interim Vice President of Finance in addition to keeping his Senior Vice President of Marketing job. The skeleton accounting department reported to him."

"So how did the scam work?"

"Jack had authority to write checks and then was involved in bank reconciliations so he could have easily covered his tracks. The financial controls at Tropical were inadequate and should have been flagged by their public accounting firm as a risk."

"We need to call Vince Truex and let him know what you discovered."

"Well, he called me earlier this afternoon and asked if I turned anything up. So I told him I found a way that Jack could have stolen from Tropical. This doesn't prove that he stole any money, rather it shows how it could have been done," said Maggie.

"What did Vince say?"

"He said the only way we could run this to ground would be by talking to Jack Heygood."

"Hopefully Vince was appreciative of your research efforts."

"Well he did say that if we ever broke up he

would like to take me out."

I laughed. "The guy is totally shameless!"

CHAPTER 24

The week before we flew to Phoenix for the NCT went by quickly. I could do some of my work at National Airlines remotely from Phoenix but I tried to work ahead on other projects that required my presence in Fort Worth. Rumors persisted about a new acquisitions project which potentially could prevent me from making the trip to Phoenix, but fortunately nothing materialized. Maggie's temporary assignment was now complete. She had arrived back in Dallas earlier in the afternoon. As soon as I returned home from work, I changed clothes and headed down the street to see her. Jim Flaw, a neighbor, was standing in the driveway with Maggie. They were looking at her house and talking with their backs towards me as Jim pointed at different parts of the house. He was a short guy with a fifty-dollar haircut.

"Hi Maggie," I said.

Maggie turned and looked a little surprised as

she had not seen me and then quickly glanced at Jim. Then she walked towards me and gave me a hug. I continued, "Just wanted to say goodbye before we left for Phoenix."

"Thanks for coming by, I hope you and the boys have a nice trip," said Maggie.

I was a little surprised by Maggie's abrupt response. I thought she would ask me in to talk but that didn't seem to be in the cards. Jim walked towards me and we shook hands.

"Maggie tells me you are going on a baseball trip to Arizona," said Jim.

"Yes, this is the final tournament of the year and I am looking forward to a little time away from baseball and spending more time with Maggie."

I then asked Jim, "How is your real estate business doing?"

"The recent up-tick in the Dallas economy has boosted sales," said Jim.

Maggie had a serious expression on her face and looked away from me. I took a couple of steps forward and gave her a hug before I turned and walked back up the street to my house.

CHAPTER 25

Mark, Josh, Joe and I left for DFW a few minutes after eight in the morning. The DART commuter train ride to the airport went smoothly. We exited DART and went into the terminal to the National Airlines passenger check-in area. After standing in line for ten minutes we checked our bags and got boarding passes. The baseball equipment bags were heavy so I had to pay $350 to ship them—bags didn't fly free on National! On our way to gate A22 we stopped to eat some breakfast tacos and the boys purchased magazines to read on the plane. Soon we were at the gate and I spotted a few old friends. The Dallas Braves had also qualified for the National Championship and would be on the same flight to Phoenix. Joe had played a few seasons with the Braves in past summers and we still had many friends on the team. I walked up to a group of Braves parents standing in line at the A22 podium. "Great to see you guys," I said.

The parent in line in front of me turned and stuck out his hand. "Mr. Jones, good to see you," he said.

"This has been a long season. Josh Baker and Mark Heygood have been at the house all summer and everyone needs a break," I said.

"We heard about Wendy Heygood and Jerry Huggins."

"It was tragic; I did what I could to support Mark after Jack disappeared."

"Yeah, the more I hear about Jack, the uglier it gets."

"Let's talk about the NCT," I said. "I just got the tournament bracket last night."

"Well, the only thing I know is that the Braves play the team from Elmira, New York in the first round."

We were now directly in front of the podium and the Braves dad received his boarding pass. "Talk to you in Phoenix. Good luck to the Generals!" Then he turned and walked to the boarding area.

I found a seat and opened the package of tournament information. There would be eight teams in this double elimination tournament: Dallas Generals, Dallas Braves, Miami Gators, Cincinnati Bombers, Elmira Giants, East Cobb Pelicans, Northern California Renegades and Bayamon Cardinales from Puerto Rico. The tournament would last five days. A total of 14 games would be played if the winning team swept the tournament or 15 games if the winner had one loss. This was an 18U championship and the Generals were the youngest team in the tournament since all of the players were 17 years old. The tournament would be held at the professional baseball spring training facility north of

Scottsdale.

As soon as I boarded the aircraft I fastened my seat belt and went to sleep. The last couple of months had not been very enjoyable with the murder of Wendy Heygood and the numerous problems created by Jerry Huggins' failed business. Wendy's murder had not been solved but the list of possible suspects had been whittled down with Sara Sorensen, Jerry Huggins and Jack Heygood now at the top of the list. Jerry paid me the $758 he owed me from the Atlanta trip earlier in the summer so at least I was clear of that mess. These problems would be behind us for a while. All we had to do was focus on baseball for the next week.

We landed at Sky Harbor, deplaned and headed to several busses that were waiting to transport the Generals' traveling party to the hotel in Scottsdale which would serve as tournament central. Forty minutes later, the buses pulled into the circular driveway in front of the hotel. Josh, Mark and Joe would share a room on the 12th floor. Before going upstairs to my room on the 10th floor I spoke to the hotel manager.

"I would like to restrict the movie access in room 1203."

"Sure, that is no problem," said the manager.

"Great," I said.

"How would you like me to restrict it?" he asked.

"Disable access to all X-rated movies."

"No problem."

"Thanks—I don't want to pay a hundred and seventy dollars for porno movies on this trip!"

The manager stopped what he was doing and gave me a funny look. Then he said, "I will take care of it, Mr. Jones."

• • •

No games were scheduled today and the Generals were going to practice under the lights at the baseball field. I took a nap and got up around 6:00 to meet James Alberts in the hotel lobby and carpool to the Generals' evening practice. We walked to my rental car and started driving north on the Pima Freeway to the field. James looked out the window and remarked, "The complex is supposed to be the Taj Mahal of the Cactus League."

"Yeah, only the Cubs' facility is close."

We drove for another ten minutes and exited the highway. The complex was five minutes to the west. We entered through the main gate and then drove around to the north side of the field to park. There was an empty parking spot next to the third base line gate so we pulled in. James and I got out of the car and started walking up the inclined ramp that led directly to the stadium.

He looked over the rail on the left side of the ramp. "There are five practice fields to the east."

The complex was immaculately manicured and all of the grass areas looked freshly mowed. "Nice that all of the games are played in the main stadium and not the minor league practice fields," I said.

Halfway up the one-hundred yard, inclined ramp, we stopped to view a large covered hitting facility and a spacious pitching practice area with six mounds. James studied the facility. "This complex is very impressive; you could get a lot of work done here during spring training."

"And we're only looking at half of it. There are five more practice fields on the other side of the main stadium for the other MLB team that shares the complex," I said as I pointed at the fields to the southwest.

We took ten mores steps and a group of baseball players appeared at the entrance to the stadium. The Miami Gators were walking down the ramp from the stadium towards their bus in the north parking lot. "So we have the Gators tomorrow," I noted.

James glanced at the players. "The Gators have a lot of talent—three were chosen in the MLB draft."

I looked at James and laughed. "Too bad they haven't signed."

In a couple of minutes the Gators passed directly in front of James and me. Most of the Gators spoke Spanish and were big and intimidating.

We continued walking and five minutes later we passed through an open gate into the main stadium where MLB teams played their spring training games. I stopped and surveyed the stadium. "Wow, what a place! Do you see the MLB team offices in the far corners of the outfield?"

"Yes, very nice. This stadium can seat over twelve thousand fans," said James as he scanned the outfield. "That's a unique hitter's eye beyond the centerfield fence. I have never seen a four-tiered hitter's eye with cacti growing in each tier."

"The design is very unique," I remarked. "I like the field layout with the sun behind home plate and the mountains in the distance behind the left field wall."

Glancing down at the field, James added, "This is a big field with center field at 420 feet, 390 feet in the alleys and 345 feet in the corners but the ball carries well in the hot, dry air."

The Generals were already on the field and set

up the L screen in front of the mound so batting practice could begin. James and I walked down several rows to have a good vantage point for my favorite part of practice. "All of the players hit the ball well in the regional at TCU. Let's hope that continues here in Scottsdale," said James.

The players took batting practice in three groups and we were midway through the second group. "How many balls have landed deep in the lawn areas behind the outfield walls?" I asked.

"I have counted twenty so far. These guys have gorilla-type power."

"We look ready to go at the plate," I said.

James looked to his right and shielded his eyes from the intense sun setting in the west. "I'm glad all the games will be at night."

"That's the only way to go in Arizona during August."

"Glad Rizzo is here; he's probably worth a couple of runs a game," said James.

"He certainly adds a lot to the staff. Sometimes I think the game moves too fast for Coach Ronny and Coach Stan."

After batting practice and a brief team meeting the Generals started their defensive drills. James smiled and pointed at the field. "I like the effort I'm seeing on the field tonight."

"With this level of competition we can't take a couple of innings off in the field like we did at TCU in the regional," I said.

The intense infield/outfield practice continued for another thirty minutes. Then the coaches huddled up with the players as the Elmira, New York team arrived on the field and started stretching before their practice.

"We need to be crisp like this in the games," said James.

Lonny nodded. "Yes, as long as we focus, we'll be good."

CHAPTER 26

Our first game in round one of the tournament was scheduled for 8:30 tonight with pregame warmups taking place in the batting cages adjacent to the field beginning at 7:00. The Generals left for the field on their bus while the remainder of the traveling party followed in a caravan of rental cars. Pete Henry, the dad of reserve player Blake Henry, hitched a ride with me to the field.

Frowning, Pete started to talk. "Lonny, I don't get it. Blake is sitting way too much. He should be playing ahead of Sorensen at third base."

Conversations with disgruntled parents about playing time were uncomfortable. I paused for a moment trying to think of the right thing to say. "Well—"

"Blake has great athletic skills," Pete interrupted. "The coaches haven't given him a fair shake."

This conversation—more of a monologue than a

conversation—continued for most of the drive to the stadium. His kid was athletically talented but a terrible hitter. Many of the dads frequently joked, "The Henry kid went zero for July!"

Pete had pearly white teeth and wore a flat top. An aggressive sales guy, he was used to getting his way. I often spotted him chirping in the coaches' ears trying to negotiate more playing time for his boy. That's the problem with select baseball—the parents have unrealistic expectations about their kids.

I turned up the volume on the car radio hoping it would drown him out but Pete continued to drone on. "Lonny, I just can't understand it. Why don't the coaches appreciate Blake's talents and get him out there on the field more?"

Finally, I couldn't keep my mouth shut any longer. "Well, Pete, Blake missed a lot games this summer when you sent him to all of those college football camps—Purdue, A&M. He never seemed to groove his swing this summer."

"Well...well..." Pete stammered, "if he would have played more, then his swing would have come back."

He wanted to say more but I continued. "The coaches expect the players to work on hitting on their own time and not use the games as batting practice. Besides, Owen Sorensen is having a hell of a season at third base—batting .382 with only two errors in fifty games. I think the coaches are going with the player that can most help the team."

Pete grimaced, shook his head, heavily inhaled and exhaled but didn't say anything. I could tell he was fuming. He wanted a shoulder to cry on but I was not the guy.

After fifteen minutes of silence, we finally arrived at the field and parked behind home plate. I sure hoped Henry would hitch a ride back to the hotel with someone else after the game.

Fortunately, Henry stopped to smoke a cigarette in the parking lot once we got out of the car and I kept on walking towards the gate. Once inside, I made my way into the stands to find my seat. Murray Sr. and his wife Sofia were standing in the aisle and waved to me to get my attention.

"Hard to believe we finally made it to Phoenix and the NCT. The boys will remember this championship tournament for the rest of their lives," Murray said. "This is a great trip for everyone."

"I love it!" Sofia beamed. "The hotel pool and bar are fantastic. We found a great Mexican restaurant a block from the hotel." Then she asked, "What about Joan? Will she come to the tournament to see Joe play? I don't think I've seen her all summer."

That was all I needed, someone asking me about my ex-wife's travel plans. Joan had shown no interest in Joe's baseball this summer and was only focused on keeping her boyfriend happy. This conversation was already starting to piss me off.

"No, she doesn't like to watch baseball and I think she told Joe that she and her boyfriend were taking a trip to Europe. Next question?" I said, trying to quickly end the conversation.

Murray Sr. could tell I was agitated and quickly walked past me and was followed by Sofia. She glanced back at me and winked. I realized she was toying with me.

●　●　●

The Miami Gators, tonight's home team, were on the field doing their pregame drills. James Alberts arrived and sat to my right one row in front of me. "I read their starting pitcher was picked in the tenth round of the June draft but hadn't signed because of the low-ball offer he received from the Phillies," said James.

I nodded. "Most of the baseball publications predicted he would be drafted in the top two rounds and sign for over one million but he fell and the Phillies offered only a hundred and fifty thousand."

James pointed at two men wearing red shirts sitting five rows in front of us. "He has something to prove and he can showcase his skills tonight with Phillies scouts in attendance."

As tonight's leadoff batter, Joe settled into the batter's box. The pitcher wound up and threw a fastball over the inner half of the plate. When Joe swung, the sharp crack of the bat drove the ball towards right field. The right fielder ran to his left and jumped but the ball was too high and passed over the top of his glove before it slammed into the wall with a thud. Joe was standing on second base for a couple of seconds before the ball was relayed in to shortstop covering the bag.

Up next, Murray McClure Jr. watched a first-pitch fastball fly over the outside corner of the plate. He must have anticipated another fastball on the second pitch since his swing was far in front and completely missed the ball as the pitcher threw a change-up for strike two. The pitcher then came back with a sizzling 93-mph fastball over the inside corner for strike three. Murray walked back to the dugout shaking his head.

Josh Baker was up next and fouled the first two

pitches off the end of his bat. Coaching third base, Ronny Espinosa gave Joe the steal sign. Joe took a three-step leadoff and broke for third while the pitcher wound up. The pitch was outside but Josh didn't swing to protect the base runner so the catcher was in an ideal position to throw down to third base. The catcher's throw was perfect—low and just inside of the bag—and Joe slid into the third baseman's glove for the second out. Josh stood in the batter's box shaking his head. The Gator pitcher came back with a curveball in the dirt that Josh helplessly swung at for strike three and the third out.

James Alberts looked away from the field and frowned. "With this competition, we need to move base runners over when they get in scoring position if we expect to win."

I nodded in agreement. "I can see why the Gators' pitcher was drafted. He changes speeds and mixes up his pitches to keep the batters off balance."

Joe was the starting pitcher for the Generals. He seemed to command all of his pitches during pregame warmup and looked like he was ready to go. The Gators had a reputation for being aggressive on the base paths and liked to challenge opposing pitchers and catchers. Today was no exception. The leadoff batter bunted the first pitch five feet down the third base line before it stopped a few inches from the chalk foul line. Catcher Brock Dillard stumbled slightly getting out of his receiving stance before he took four steps and fielded the bunt. His throw was off target to the left of first base and pulled Mark Heygood off the bag. The batter was safe and for some unexplained reason credited with a hit.

The Gators' second batter took the first pitch as the runner on first base broke to steal second. Dillard was in an ideal position to throw the runner out but his throw flew over the outstretched glove of the shortstop, Tyrone Alberts, covering second base, and into center field enabling the base runner to advance to third with no outs.

Joe briefly fidgeted on the mound and glanced home towards Brock. His next pitch was a biting curveball that the batter flared into right field. Murray McClure Jr. broke for the ball with his blinding speed and made a highlight-film, diving catch near the right field line before somersaulting into the wall. The runner at third tagged up and sprinted towards home plate while Murray scrambled back to his feet. The throw from Murray to Brock Owen was not in time and the runner scored standing up. Without any base runners to distract him, Joe was able to strike the next two batters out on a good mix of fastballs and change-ups.

The remainder of the game turned into a defensive struggle as little offense was generated due to the outstanding pitching performances from both teams. Joe looked good and went the distance for the Generals, giving up four hits and one run but that was not enough to beat the Gators and prevent the Generals from losing their first game in the double-elimination tournament. However, I noticed the scouts took plenty of notes while Joe pitched since this sort of performance from a seventeen-year-old kid was pretty impressive. Hopefully, Joe's outing improved his stock with college coaches and gave him some visibility with the professional scouts before the draft next year. The Philadelphia draftee pitched the game of his life for the Gators and limited the Generals to only three hits and no runs. That performance likely positioned him to negotiate a lucrative deal with the Phillies at the conclusion of the NCT. There would be no more room for error by the Generals or we would be flying back to Dallas. Once teams were eliminated, NCT officials usually booked them on the next available departing flight from Phoenix to their hometown.

The Generals held a team meeting in the parking lot immediately after the game. Mike Rizzo appeared very displeased and lectured the boys for twenty minutes. I was not surprised when he immediately scheduled an 8:00 batting practice at Scottsdale Chaparral High School the following morning.

CHAPTER 27

After the traveling party returned to the hotel the stunned Generals parents congregated in the pool bar to discuss what had just happened on the diamond. The competition was even better than we had expected. Going forward, it was apparent that all of the players would need to be at the top of their games if we were going to be a factor in the NCT.

After a couple of beers, it was time for me to get some sleep and I headed through the main lobby to the elevator bank. I passed the front desk and was surprised to see a familiar figure—Nick Del Monico, the lawyer from Lubbock. He and another man were standing in line to check in to the hotel. I tried to avoid eye contact with Nick but he saw me and shouted out a greeting, "Well, well, Mr. Jones."

I could not gracefully escape so I walked over to Nick and stuck out my hand.

"Mr. Jones, I want you to meet Butch Baker," said Nick. "Butch and I just drove in from Lubbock.

FASTBALL

We're here to watch the NCT."

Butch Baker stood 6'0" and probably weighed 245 pounds. He was solid muscle and tough looking.

Butch smiled as he shook my hand. "Lonny, I'm sorry I wasn't able to meet with you when you flew out to Lubbock. Josh very much enjoys staying with you and Joe in Dallas. I appreciate your help."

"Our pleasure," I responded. "We enjoy having Josh stay with us."

"Nick and I plan to have a card game at a table in the pool bar area later this evening. We could save a seat for you Lonny," said Butch.

"What are you boys playing?" I asked.

"Texas hold 'em."

Since I loved to play poker I thought about the invitation for a minute but quickly remembered that Butch's current legal woes in Lubbock were due to a brawl after a card game. After getting an up-close look at Butch, I realized any altercation with him would not have a happy ending.

"Butch, I appreciate the offer but I need to get some rack, it's been a very long day."

"Lonny, let's talk about this," he said, and I could smell the alcohol on his breath. "We will only play for a couple of hours and you will be back in your room by one o'clock, no later."

"We'll limit the betting to twenty dollars per hand," added Nick. "A shoe salesman and a doctor have already agreed to play."

"Okay, okay, you've talked me into it."

We met thirty minutes later at the pool bar and sat down at a table in the corner. The shoe salesman was in his late 30s, bald and overweight, while the doctor looked trim and in his early 60s. We all ordered drinks while Butch shuffled the cards.

Butch looked well practiced as he adroitly handled the deck of cards. Then he spread the cards face down on the table so we could draw to determine the first dealer. Not surprisingly to me, Butch held the high card, a J ♠, so he would have the dealer button first. Nick sat to Butch's left followed by the doctor, shoe salesman and myself seated directly to the right of Butch. He dealt everyone two hole cards. I discretely lifted my hole cards and saw that I was holding a 9 ♦ and 9 ♠ – not a bad starting hand. Just then the drinks arrived; the doctor and I had light beers while everyone else drank whisky neat.

As we sipped our drinks, I provided Butch an update on the tournament. "Since the Generals lost tonight we are now in the losers bracket and we don't play tomorrow. Batting practice is scheduled for eight o'clock tomorrow morning over at Chaparral High School."

Butch shook his head in disbelief. "We lost our opener?"

"Yes, the pitcher on the Gators was dominating."

"How did Josh do?"

"I think he had three at-bats: a strikeout on a curveball in the dirt and then two line drives to right field that were caught."

"He needs to do better than that. Now is the time to negotiate a good deal," said Butch with an irritated expression on his face.

Nick raised his eyebrows with a concerned look and said, "Let's get back to cards."

None of the players expressed any emotion as they reviewed their hole cards. Only the doctor folded during the flop round of betting. Butch dealt the first three community cards: 5 ♦, Q ♣ and 2 ♥. I still only had one pair. Betting continued after both the fourth community card, 6 ♣, and fifth community card, 3 ♠, were dealt and everyone except the doctor had placed $20 in the pot. It was time for the showdown. Nick's hole cards were 5 ♥ and 6 ♦ so he had two pairs. The shoe salesman showed Q ♦ and Q ♠ so he had three Qs. I had one pairs of 9s. Butch frowned as he revealed his hole cards, 5 ♥ and 5 ♣, so he had three 5s. The shoe salesman had won the $80 pot.

After two more games, Butch and I were each down $60, the doctor was down $40, Nick was up $40 and the shoe salesman was up $120. It was apparent that Butch was becoming increasingly frustrated with the shoe salesman since he was up $120 and would frequently need to be reminded of the value of the pot which slowed the game down. On another occasion, the shoe salesman's money became intermingled with the pot so the game was momentarily stopped as we sorted it out. I didn't feel his actions were deliberate but rather a consequence of the late hour and multiple rounds of whisky. Now he had the button so it was his turn to deal the next game. His first two clumsy attempts to shuffle the deck had to be repeated as some of the cards landed face up. As the shoe salesman dealt the hole cards, Butch stood and screamed at him, "You cheating son of a bitch!"

Immediately, the shoe salesman got up out of his seat and took a wild roundhouse swing at Butch that missed his head by a foot. Unfortunately, I was seated between two drunken men that were getting ready to throw down. I quickly stood and put one hand on each of them to keep them apart. "Guys, guys, guys...c'mon now," I said.

After a few intense seconds, both Butch and the

shoe salesman sat back down and laughed. I looked at my watch. "Gentlemen, it is two-fifteen and time for me to hit the sack," I said as I gathered up what little was left of my cash and pushed my chair under the table.

"Lonny, it's been fun, see you at the field in the morning," said Butch with a big grin on his face.

The bartender was the only other person remaining in the bar. He shook his head and gave me a nod as I exited the pool area. The lobby was deserted as I made my way to the elevator bank and up to my room for some badly needed sleep.

CHAPTER 28

The Scottsdale Chaparral High School baseball field was located off of Gold Dust Avenue directly west of the high school. As usual, all of the players arrived ten minutes early for practice and assembled on the field. At precisely 8:00 Mike gathered the boys around and addressed the team. The meeting was only for coaches and players and took place near second base away from the parents observing from the stands. It was a no-nonsense meeting and you could tell that Mike had the players' complete attention.

The players hit against both right-handed and left-handed pitching. Mike Rizzo was left-handed and threw the first round. Each batter executed three bunts and then tried to hit the next ten pitches to the opposite field. Finally, each batter swung away at the next ten pitches. Once all of the Generals had batted the coaches flipped the L-screen and Coach Stan White repeated the same process while throwing right-handed.

A few minutes later several scouts walked into the stands and took seats to observe the Generals' practice. Radar guns immediately appeared and laptops opened. These scouts had not attended any of the Generals' games in Dallas or at elite tournaments across the country so I didn't know if they were college or professional baseball scouts. Then Nick Del Monico and Butch Baker arrived in the red Corvette and walked into the stands. Butch and Nick immediately made their way down to the field and spoke to Coach Ronny Espinosa who was standing on the side of the field near the fence. I was close enough that I could hear parts of their conversation.

Ronny extended his hand to both men and said, "Butch, glad you were able to come to the tournament. How was the drive from Lubbock?"

Butch smiled and responded, "Well, Nick was finally able to get me out of jail before my trial. The judge is a baseball fan and agreed to let me leave Lubbock and attend the tournament. We broke every speed limit and made it here in a little less than ten hours."

Then Ronny, Butch and Nick turned and looked up at the stands. Butch asked, "Which of the scouts do I need to talk to?"

"The guy with the red shirt and white golf hat told me he was very interested in Josh," said Ronny.

"We need to find out if we can get a better deal than the Oklahoma Tech offer that is already on the table," added Butch.

Nick interjected, "The deal I struck with Tech was very lucrative—cash for you and the Corvette for Josh. I'd be surprised if we could do any better."

Butch appeared to be annoyed at those words. "Listen, Nick, I know you are a Tech guy but I want to hear what people will offer so I can make the best decision for Josh."

Coach Espinosa interrupted. "You know, Josh told me he wanted to go to Los Angeles to play both football and baseball at California Southern University."

Butch gritted his teeth and had a kind of wild look on his face. "Guys, all of that talk about Tech and Los Angeles took place while I was in jail. Now that I am out I will be calling the shots. Is that clear?"

Both Ronny and Nick backed up a step, unsure what was going to happen next. The conversation was over. Butch turned and headed into the stands towards the man with the red shirt and white golf hat closely followed by Nick Del Monico.

CHAPTER 29

Our first opponent in the round-two losers bracket would be the Bayamon Cardinales from Puerto Rico. Bayamon is located on the Puerto Rican coast just west of San Juan and has a history of producing professional baseball players. Joe played in a tournament in Bayamon when he was twelve years old and we traveled by school bus from our hotel in downtown San Juan to the stadium each day. His team finished as runner-up to the Puerto Rican all-star team. I wondered if any of the players from that all-star team would play for the Cardinales.

The Cardinales were home team and took the field first. Their pitcher was left-handed and seemed to favor throwing curveballs in the pregame warmups. The game started and our leadoff batter Tyrone Alberts walked on four straight balls thrown by the Cardinales pitcher. Up next, Joe drove a double down the right field line that plated Alberts. Then Josh batted and was promptly hit by the first pitch. The Cardinales pitcher sensed he was in trouble and started looking towards his dugout. Their coaches shouted words of encouragement to the pitcher in Spanish but did not visit the mound to calm him down.

Murray Jr. settled into the batter's box to wait for his first pitch. The pitcher hung a curveball that Murray Jr. smashed straight at the shortstop. The ball was hit hard and took a funny bounce in the infield grass that caused the path of the ball to change. The shortstop elected not to get in front of the ball to block it with his body and instead tried to play it with his backhand. The ball shot past him into left field and both base runners scored. The Cardinales were down 0-3 with no outs in the first inning. The next two batters from the Generals managed to get on base due to fielding errors by the second baseman and the pitcher. The Cardinales were now in complete disarray. The Generals scored three more runs in the first and the rout was on. The Cardinales hung their heads and were unfocused for the remainder of the game. By the third inning, the Cardinales dugout was completely silent. They would be on the 8:30 a.m. nonstop flight back to San Juan the next day.

The Generals were excited to win their first game and still be alive in the NCT. Tomorrow's game in round three would pit them against the Northern California Renegades who lost to the Bombers in the winners bracket. Everyone soon returned to the hotel and the players jumped into the large rectangular swimming pool. Most of the parents congregated at the pool bar and I noticed Butch Baker and Nick Del Monico playing cards with a couple of dads from the Elmira, New York

team that I had met the previous day. They kept
their money out of sight but you could feel the
intensity of the game from twenty feet away. I
walked by on my way to my room and stopped to say
hi to Nick and Butch.

"How are you boys doing?" I asked.

Butch's eyes never left the cards on the table as
he said, "It's great to still be alive at the NCT!"

Nick added, "The Cardinales were completely
outclassed. I bet the Northern California Renegades
will not fold like a cheap suitcase."

I had seen Butch conversing with numerous
scouts at our game but didn't know if he had finally
determined where Josh would further his education
after high school.

"Butch, have you guys committed to a college?" I
asked.

"Nope, not yet, we're hoping for a better offer—I
mean better opportunity—before we make a final
decision."

Butch noticed that Nick Del Monico winced at
those words and then started to laugh. "Nick, come
on now, it will be okay. It's just business."

The dads from the Elmira team had quizzical
looks on their faces while Nick said nothing and
grimaced. A long, awkward silence passed before
Butch laughed and added, "Playing cards at the pool
in Scottsdale sure beats sitting in the Lubbock
County Jail."

He roared with laughter and took a drink of his
whisky neat. The Elmira dads exchanged glances
and looked even more confused. Evidently, they had
never met a guy like Butch Baker before.

As I turned and started to leave, Butch said,
"Lonny, how would you like to play some cards with

a couple of Elmira's finest?"

"I'm still trying to recover from the game with the shoe salesman the other night so I better pass, but thanks for asking."

CHAPTER 30

Every game in the losers bracket could be sudden death for the Generals. Now in round three, the players and coaches appeared to be totally focused on our next game against the Renegades. I knew a little about the Renegades. A couple of their players were highly recruited and had committed to play baseball at Stanford. Their starting pitcher stood 6'4" and had great command of a variety of pitches. We briefly saw him pitch in the Renegades' opening game and his fastball had good velocity but I didn't see a lot of movement on the ball. Their third baseman was good sized and had a lot of pop in his bat. Both of these players would likely make a major impact on the Stanford baseball program for years to come.

The Generals were once again the visiting team so the Renegades took the field to start the game. The first four innings went by quickly as both starting pitchers had dominating performances and no batters reached base. In the top of the fifth inning Josh led off followed by Murray Jr. We needed to score some runs. Josh took the first two pitches, which were both balls off the outside of the plate. The Renegades pitcher then threw a 95-mph pitch on the inside corner of the plate; Josh turned on the ball and hit a moon-shot homerun over the right field wall. He trotted around the bases and all of the Generals came out of the dugout to congratulate him after he stepped on home plate. Butch Baker, seated three rows in front of me, tried to stand but stumbled and his flask fell to the ground. Soon he was on his feet screaming, "Bomb time! Bomb time!"

All of the Generals parents were standing as Murray Jr. settled into the batter's box while some of the Generals were still returning to the dugout. The pitcher was upset and didn't wait for everyone to get in the dugout. He fired a 94-mph fastball over the heart of the plate. Murray Jr.'s bat connected perfectly with the ball and hit a sizzling line drive over the right field fence. Two fastballs were hit back to back over the fence. Shocked, the Renegades pitcher looked over to his dugout. The coach sensed he needed a break to regroup and immediately headed to the mound for a visit after calling time out.

All of the Renegades' infielders and the coach converged on the mound for a visit. After a brief conversation, the coach signaled for another pitcher to come into the game. The starter had enough of the Generals' bats and was done for the day.

The relief pitcher was not as dominating as the starter and the Generals were able to score three more runs in the remaining two innings while holding the Renegades to two runs. The Generals won the game 5-2 and would continue to advance in the tournament. Only four teams now remained alive in the tournament: the undefeated East Cobb Pelicans and the once-defeated Bombers, Giants and Generals.

CHAPTER 31

Pairings in round four of the tournament were not as straightforward as they had been in the earlier rounds. The pairings for the remainder of the tournament would be determined by Rule 162 in the NCT Official Handbook. At this point of the tournament, Rule 162's only impact would be that teams would not play teams previously played unless there were only two teams alive in the tournament. The NCT Tournament officials determined that the Pelicans would play the Elmira Giants while the Generals would face the Cincinnati Bombers that were previously beaten by the Pelicans.

The Cincinnati Bombers had established a reputation for having one of the premier baseball programs in the county. The Bombers had won the NCT Tournament several times in the past and recruited players from across the country. Their recruiting reach far exceeded the Generals and their alumni included some of the top professional baseball players.

The Generals would play the second game of the evening that would commence thirty minutes after the conclusion of the Pelicans vs. Giants game. After batting practice was completed in the cages behind the right field stands, the Generals watched the conclusion of the earlier game. The Pelicans were ahead 5-0 and appeared in complete control during the final two innings. Whichever team survived in the finale tonight would have their hands full playing the Pelicans in the championship game tomorrow.

Then the Bombers and Generals assembled on the field for a brief warmup before their game. Fifteen minutes later the umpires summoned the opposing coaches to home plate for the coin toss. The Bombers won the coin toss and elected to be the home team. Bomber pitching was dominant during the first six innings as the Generals were only able to score one run. However, the Generals made several uncharacteristic errors that enabled the Bombers to lead by a score of 3-1 going into the last inning. Since we were the visiting team we needed to score at least two runs to tie the game or go ahead to avoid immediate elimination. At the top of the seventh inning Mark Heygood and Tyrone Alberts were able to get on base with singles but were followed by two strikeouts. Juan Francisco was next to bat. The Generals needed some offense now. However, so far tonight Juan had gone 0-3 at the plate with two strikeouts. Juan's family was seated in the row of seats directly in front of me yelling words of encouragement to him in Spanish. Juan took the first pitch for a called strike and you could hear a collective sigh from the Francisco family. The pitcher decided to throw the same exact pitch on his next throw and Juan was ready. Juan swung and lifted a ball directly down the right field line that was over the outfield fence and two feet inside the foul pole for a three-run homerun that gave the Generals a 4-3 lead. The Generals fans were on their feet screaming and giving each other high-fives. The Francisco family was delirious and did a group hug. The Generals were now up 4-3. Our next batter was thrown out on a slow, three-hop grounder to the second baseman so we proceeded to the bottom of the seventh inning with a one-run lead. The Bombers would get their last at-bats.

The first Bomber to bat in the seventh inning blasted the first pitch to the base of the centerfield wall. It was a great shot but Joe made the routine catch on the warning track next to the 400-foot sign for the first out. Up next, the Bomber batter took the first pitch for a ball but singled the next pitch into left field. The third Bomber batter turned on the first pitch and blasted the ball to the third base side of shortstop Alberts who took two steps to his right and then dived to field the ball. He quickly got to his feet, turned and fired to Francisco at second base who then threw over to Mark Heywood at first base. It was a perfectly executed double play to end the game. The Generals had punched their ticket for a date with East Cobb in the championship game.

After the game, several parents briefly assembled in the parking lot to recap the victory and discuss dinner options. Murray Sr. said, "Let's try the sushi place across the street from the hotel. I'm getting a little tired of Mexican food and steaks."

Brock Dillard's mother nodded. "That's a good

idea. Maybe some of the coaches would like to join us. Let me talk to Ronny."

I raised my eyebrows slightly as I had a flashback of seeing her and Coach Ronny alone in the swimming pool in Marietta. Apparently, only Coach Stan and I had witnessed that display of passion since nobody had ever mentioned it. Another affair between two single parents quickly became common knowledge after it was discovered. The majority of parents were fairly straight-laced and frowned upon what they viewed as unethical behavior but I tried not to be judgmental and usually minded my own business. After a brief discussion, Murray Sr., Sofia, Brock Dillard's mother, Juan Francisco's parents and I agreed to meet at the sushi restaurant across the street from the hotel at 8:00.

Murray Sr., Sofia and I were the first to arrive at the restaurant and secured a table. We were quickly followed by the Francisco parents and Brock Dillard's mother accompanied by Ronny Espinosa. We ordered Japanese beer and the discussion quickly turned to the unanswered questions surrounding the Heygoods.

"Lonny, everyone really appreciates your taking care of Mark Heygood during the baseball season. What will happen to him after the season?" asked Brock Dillard's mother.

"I'm in regular contact with Jack's sister, Sharon, in Oklahoma City. She agreed to let Mark stay with Joe, Josh and me for the remainder of the season. Later this month, Mark will move to Oklahoma City. Sharon has already enrolled him in a private school for his senior year of high school."

Sofia quickly scanned the menu. "Shall we order

some appetizers that we could share?"

We pondered the appetizer section of the menu for a few minutes and then Sofia said, "What sounds good?"

"I vote for spicy tuna, shrimp tempura and salmon avocado rolls," I said.

Coach Ronny nodded approvingly and added, "Let's also get the sampler with dumplings, chicken yakitori, kalbi and calamari."

"That sounds fantastic," said Murray, Sr.

Soon the appetizers and the next round of beer arrived. For a few minutes everyone was heads-down devouring the appetizers before the conversation returned to the Heygoods.

"Has their house sold yet?" inquired Sofia.

I finished chewing a piece of calamari and then said, "It was priced to sell and there is a contract on it. I think the deal will likely close in a couple of weeks."

We quickly finished the appetizers and several people started to study the entrée options.

"That was delicious. What shall we order for the main course?" asked Pedro Francisco.

Sofia pointed at page three of the menu. "Take a look at the combinations on the bottom of third page. They look good."

Coach Ronny looked up from the menu. "The mega boat combination looks outstanding. The tuna, salmon and yellow tail sashimi sound great."

"Plus all of the sushi and rolls," I added.

We soon placed the order and the miso soup was served a few minutes ahead of the other food. Sipping her soup, Sofia looked up and said, "This is very tasty."

Brock Dillard's mother glanced at me for a few

seconds and waited for a break in the conversation before she asked, "What about Wendy's murder? Are the police any closer to solving it?"

Everyone stopped eating and looked at me. The table became silent.

"Detective Truex questioned me at length around the time of the murder but we have had very limited contact recently. I think he may have some soft leads that lack motives. He did mention he had flown down to West Palm Beach to look for Jack and was unable to locate him but he did find out that Jack has been playing house with a promiscuous bar waitress in Delray Beach."

Sofia laughed. "I wonder how long that was going on. I always thought Jack was a player."

I glimpsed out of the corner of my eye at Coach Ronny and Brock's mother and saw them exchange uncomfortable glances.

Finally, after fifteen minutes, everyone stopped eating and there was still fish on the platters. I was completely full. After a brief discussion we decided to skip dessert and then walked back to the hotel across the street.

CHAPTER 32

After dropping their first game to the Miami Gators, the Generals were having a great tournament. Three straight victories had put us in the first championship game against the undefeated East Cobb Pelicans. If we lost the next day then East Cobb would be champions; if the Generals won the first championship game then both teams would have one loss and there would be a second championship game immediately following the first game. The winner would be the champion. We had to win these two games!

I returned to my room after the sushi dinner. Finding nothing interesting on TV, I decided to have a beer at the wet bar near the pool and talk with some of the other parents before retiring. I stepped off the elevator in the lobby. The Cincinnati Bombers had assembled with their equipment and luggage, and would soon be boarding busses to Sky Harbor to catch their red-eye flight home to Cincinnati.

I ran into Mike Rizzo on my way to the pool. "Mike, thank you for giving Joe the opportunity to play on your team this year. It has been a great experience."

"It was my pleasure to have Joe play on the Generals this season. He's a great young man. You've done a great job raising him," reflected Mike.

"Thank you very much, Mike. Hopefully we can play with the Generals next summer before Joe starts college."

"Has Joe made a decision regarding college?"

"We thought he was a lock for LSU after the Atlanta trip but their interest has cooled in the last month after a pitcher from Georgia committed to them."

"Would you like me to make some calls and see what I can come up with?"

"Thank you Mike, that would be very much appreciated! If possible, Joe would like to play in the Big 12 or SEC."

I shook hands with Mike and continued walking towards the pool bar to socialize with the other parents for a few minutes.

Soon it was 11 p.m. and time for me to get some rest. Many of the other parents encouraged me to stay at the bar and continue to party but I needed some sleep so I headed up to my room on the 10th floor. It was difficult to get to sleep since I was pumped up about the championship game but I finally dozed off before midnight.

About 2:00 I heard a loud knock at my door. I was groggy and it took me several seconds to react. Who could it be? Probably some drunk had the wrong room. The knocking continued. Maybe it was Joe? I got out of bed, walked to the door and looked through the peephole but only saw the outline of a person that I could not identify. The knocking continued.

Finally I yelled, "Who the hell is it?"

"It's Jack—Jack Heygood from Dallas."

I opened the door and there he was. He looked much older than I remembered. His face was sunburned and his hair was partially gray. Jack didn't wait for me to invite him in as he quickly walked past me into my room.

"Shut the door!" he exclaimed. "I drove in from Texas to see Mark play but I think someone started following me after I left the Generals' game this evening."

Jack's eyes flashed from side to side and he was breathing hard. He walked over to the window and looked outside through the slit in the drapes. Then he turned and looked at me with a helpless expression on his face.

"Lonny, you are the only guy I could go to," he said.

"Did anyone follow you to the hotel tonight?" I asked.

"No, no, I think I lost them a couple of hours ago. Please let me stay here tonight until I figure out my next move."

I could not believe he had the balls to make that request. I wanted to throw his ass out into the hallway. This was the same guy who ran away when I got into the dust-up with the two thugs in the parking lot during the season opener.

"Okay, okay, but only tonight. I am only doing this because I like your kid. Don't expect me to help you out if there is any trouble. You're on your own now after you left me to take your beating in the parking lot at the baseball field."

"Lonny, I was scared and lost my head, I thought they were going to kill me."

Jack laid down on the couch and shut his eyes. He appeared completely exhausted. He had some explaining to do if he was going to be given refuge in my room. I walked over and shook him.

"Jack, why did you do it? Why did you screw so many people out of their life savings?"

Jack sat up and started talking fast. "It wasn't easy; I felt terrible. The chairman of Tropical Investments, William Clayton, cooked up the scheme to tide us over for a short period—maybe a year at the most. But things didn't work out and everything spiraled out of control."

"Why didn't you just walk away from Tropical?"

"I wanted to leave the company years ago and talked it over with Wendy."

Jack took a couple of deep breaths and then continued. "She told me to tough it out and things would turn around. Wendy didn't want us to lose my salary and bonus. We both made a lot of money but were spending it at a very high rate. We were living like high-rollers. She made a little over two hundred thousand per year but that paled in comparison to my salary and bonus package that was north of a million per year. Without my compensation, we would need to sell a couple of our homes and the boat. We had a home in Vail. Our boat was moored in Annapolis close to the condo. Wendy expected me to suck it up. She warned me that if I quit Tropical Investments then I would need to move my ass out of her house."

"What did she say when the company went belly-up?"

"It took several months for Wendy to believe that Tropical would not miraculously rebound and become solvent. Then she got mad."

Jack shook his head and sighed. "Wendy called me a loser and told me to get out of the house since she was wasting her time with a bum like me."

With a shrug, he raised his hands. He didn't know what else to say.

"Jack, before you start to feel too sorry for yourself, Detective Truex went to Florida and talked to your mistress Sunny."

"Okay, you found out I had some action on the side, so what. Wendy was wound way too tight for me and I needed a change."

"How can you afford to make house payments in Dallas and keep a mistress in Delray Beach after the trustee clawed back your Tropical bonuses and salaries?"

Jack just looked at me and smiled. "I don't know what you are getting at, Lonny."

"Yes you do. I think you had a nice opportunity to steal from Tropical Investments when you were writing checks and then doing the bank reconciliations. I bet the other senior guys didn't even know you were working that scam."

Jack nodded. "Lonny, that is pretty thoughtful investigative work, how did you put that together?"

"It seemed like the best opportunity for you to steal from Tropical Investments was to exploit the weakened accounting controls caused by the headcount reductions in finance and accounting. So why did you steal?"

Jack paused for a moment, raised his hands and said, "The other senior guys were getting bigger bonuses so I needed to do something to level the field. None of the other senior officers ever suspected a thing while Tropical Investments was still operating."

"The FBI must have done a pretty sloppy investigation to miss this."

"They didn't miss it. The federal prosecutor wanted to put William Clayton in jail for a long time. I had the information that would make all of the charges stick so my lawyer negotiated total immunity for every crime I committed at Tropical Investments."

As I shook my head in total disbelief, I said, "So you didn't go to jail and left Tropical with a nice nest egg—unbelievable."

Jack laughed. "Yeah, I am a winner."

I had one last question for Jack. "So what happened to Wendy? Do you know who killed her?"

"Yeah, I think I do. The day before she was murdered a couple of guys from New York contacted me and said they knew I had been stealing money from Tropical accounts for many years. They wanted to meet me at the house the next day to collect the money."

"Who were those guys?" I asked.

"They claimed to represent a couple of investors who lost millions of dollars on their investment in Tropical. Those were the same guys that beat me up at the Generals' opening game. They said if I didn't give them at least three hundred thousand dollars they were going to introduce me to a lug wrench. I was scared; those guys look pretty mean and do this kind of work for a living."

"So what happened the next day when Wendy was murdered?"

"I went to the house a couple of hours before

they were supposed to arrive to talk to Wendy about my problem. I was hoping she would agree to let me use the funds left that were hidden at the house."

"Did she give you the money?" I asked.

"She laughed at me and said it was my problem. Then she told me to get out of her house and never return."

"What happened next?"

"I went upstairs and packed a suitcase with as much of my clothing as I could fit in it and left."

"Did you tell Wendy that the New York guys were coming to the house and expected to be paid that afternoon?"

"No, Wendy was the bitch that forced me to continue to work at Tropical after I wanted to quit. She was the reason we were in this mess. I thought she deserved whatever she got. I thought they were just going to slap her around. Maybe things got out of hand?"

Jack appeared exhausted and then laid down again and quickly went to sleep on the couch. Why did Jack have to come to my room and visit me with these burdens? I could easily become collateral damage if the New York guys had followed Jack to the hotel.

There was nothing interesting on TV so I turned out the lights and spent the next two hours trying to sleep with one eye open and finally nodded off around 4:00. I was in a deep sleep and started to dream. In my dream I could hear someone playing with the lock on the door then I thought I heard footsteps.

"Oh shit," I exclaimed—it wasn't a dream. Someone had just walked into the room.

"What do you want?" I said.

I started to get up from the bed but stopped when I realized I was looking up at the business end of a sawed-off shotgun. I raised my hands. A second person entered the room and started beating Jack. The big guy holding the shotgun looked at me closely and spoke with a heavy New York accent, "You're the hero from the parking lot. I am going to cancel your ticket if you don't do exactly what I say."

"Okay, okay," I quickly responded.

Soon Jack was tied up and gagged with duct tape. Hopefully, they were not planning to take both Jack and me since the result would be fairly predictable. I didn't want to end up under the interstate highway system or go through a wood shredder.

The big guy waved his gun menacingly at me and said, "If you stick your face outside of this room in the next five minutes then you are a dead man."

I just nodded and kept my hands in the air. Fortunately, they soon backed out of the room with just Jack. I stayed in the room, turned on all of the lights and called hotel security. The furniture was out of place and turned over and I spotted an open package of Marlboros under the couch where Jack slept. By the time security reached my room Jack and the two thugs were long gone. This was likely the last time I would ever see or hear from Jack Heygood.

Since it was in the middle of the night and there had been no gunfire or loud noise in my room, the other guests at the hotel were oblivious to Jack's arrival and his subsequent abduction. Did it make any sense to alert the Generals and their parents now? Could it wait? The Generals had some real mojo now after winning four straight games so why screw that up? Don't mess with the cha cha! We were playing for the championship today.

I decided I would tell the Generals and their parents about Jack after we finished the tournament. There would be plenty of time to mourn the likely loss of Jack Heygood later. Then I threw on some shorts and went downstairs to the poolside restaurant to have some coffee and eggs and watch the sun rise. I looked at my watch when I finished breakfast and it was 6:30. It was time to call Jack's sister, Sharon Stephens, in Oklahoma City. I dialed her number and she immediately answered.

"Lonny, thank you for calling. How's Mark?"

"Mark is fine and having a good tournament. Sharon, I want to talk to you about something else; I want to talk to you about Jack."

"What about Jack?"

I paused for a moment so my words would come out right.

"Jack came to my room in the middle of the night. He said he was being chased by two people who wanted money. He wanted to hide in the room."

Sharon gasped and said, "Oh no! I'm so sorry he got you involved again."

"The two men must have followed him to my room because they broke in two hours after he arrived."

"Oh no, is Jack okay?"

"I don't know," I said. "They dragged him out of the room and left the hotel."

There was a long pause and then I heard a bang—like Sharon dropped the phone.

"He could be dead," she said and started to cry.

"The police are looking for him now but I haven't heard anything."

"Does Mark know about this?" she asked.

"No, not yet. I'm thinking about telling him after our final game this evening. Is that okay with you?"

"Yes, if you think that's best."

"I'm not sure how Mark will take this news. Could you meet Mark at DFW Airport tomorrow morning when we return from Arizona?"

"Certainly, we'll be there. Thanks for everything, Lonny."

CHAPTER 33

It was game time and the Generals took the field since they were the home team. There were probably 6,000 people in the stands and the seats behind home plate were filled with college and pro scouts. What an atmosphere for a youth baseball championship! Joe was on the mound and I felt pretty good because of the pitch command he displayed in the bullpen before the game.

My cell phone rang. "Hi buddy, I have been following the Generals on the Internet." The voice sounded familiar.

"Is this Jerry Huggins?"

"Yes it is. How are we looking for the championship games today? I was able to watch all of the earlier games on web TV."

"Jerry, you are a horse's ass," I said.

"Ha ha, c'mon Lonny, tell me how we're looking," said Jerry.

"Our pitching lines up well for the first game but

the coaches may need to get creative in the second game."

"Why is that?" asked Jerry.

"We don't have many fresh arms. I need to go now." When the National Anthem started to play I ended the call with Jerry.

Jerry said, "Good luck, Lonny," as I hung up my phone.

The Generals finished their pregame warmups in a few minutes and then the game started. Joe struck out the first two batters using a variety of pitches to hit the corners of the strike zone and effectively changed speeds to confuse the batters. The third batter for East Cobb was 18 years old and had been picked in the first round of the MLB draft by the Twins a month ago. He was a stud with lots of power. Joe mistakenly challenged him with a fastball on the first pitch. The batter turned on it and hit a majestic shot towards the centerfield fence. The ball sailed over the fence and bounced in the grass viewing area beyond. We were down 1-0.

Both defenses played well over the next several innings. The middle of our lineup manufactured a run in the fifth inning to tie the game by playing small ball. We entered the seventh inning deadlocked 1-1. Josh had relieved Joe on the mound and was pitching with authority. He was a power pitcher that touched 100 mph with his four-seam fastball and the East Cobb players didn't have the bat speed to hit it. They knew what was coming but couldn't do anything about it.

I glanced at the professional scouts. They were taking copious notes after every pitch Josh threw. Josh would be high on the scouts' watch list as they prepared for next year's draft. I spoke to the Giants' scout and he intimated that Josh would likely be a first-round selection if he could maintain this level of play.

Since we were the home team we had the last bat in the final inning. Joe led off with a bunt single that surprised the Pelicans. The next two batters struck out and then Josh was up. The Pelicans called time out and there was a coaching visit to the mound. Their strategy was clear as they intentionally walked Josh; somebody else besides Josh was going to have to beat them. Then Murray Jr. walked to the batter's box. Joe had advanced to third on a couple of steals and conferred with Mike Rizzo. Murray Jr. was a right-handed batter and the Pelican coach signaled his team to shift the defense towards left field to protect if he pulled the ball. The shortstop moved forty feet into left field while the second baseman played on the left side of the bag. The third baseman had to play next to the bag to hold Joe. This left a huge hole on the right side of the infield. The shift surprised me; their scouting report was wrong—Murray Jr. liked to slap the ball to the opposite field. On the second pitch, Murray Jr. hit a line drive to right field to score Joe and win the game. There would be a 30-minute break for the players to rest before the second championship game commenced.

Mike Rizzo and the Generals' coaches huddled out on the field so they could talk lineups and strategy in private away from the players and fans. The pitching decision loomed. James Alberts was seated directly to my right and he started to chat. "The tournament has been brutal on the pitching staff."

"We've played five games and lots of runs have

been scored against us," I added.

"Everybody on the pitching staff has already thrown."

James nodded. "There aren't many good options."

"The top end of our pitching staff has high pitch counts and tired arms."

"They're going to have to go with a less-talented arm and hope Josh has something left in the tank to close the game," said James as he looked at Josh standing on the dugout steps.

Ten minutes prior to the start of the game the coaching staff decided that Jose Ramirez from Mesquite, who was recently added to the tournament roster, would get the start. Jose had previously pitched against the Generals in a select league game in Dallas and showed good stuff—which was noted by the Generals' coaches—until his team unraveled under the pressure of small ball. Jose's arm was fresh since he last pitched two innings of mop-up action two weeks ago in the NCT Regional Tournament at TCU in Fort Worth. If Jose kept cool, he would be effective.

I turned to James and said, "This Ramirez kid showed some good stuff early in the game against us at Thomas Jefferson. If he gets out of the first inning okay, he should be fine."

"Let's hope so," said James.

As the visiting team, the Generals batted first. The Pelicans trotted out a right-handed, Florida signee to start the game who was highly rated with a mature approach. Joe batted first and led off with a walk after an eight-pitch at-bat. Tyrone Alberts had been moved up to the second spot in the lineup because of his recent offensive heroics. He didn't disappoint as he tripled to deep center field. The ball caromed off the top of the centerfield wall away from the outfielders, enabling Joe to score. We were up 1-0! Three strikeouts followed so now we had to play defense.

Their leadoff hitter was the same player who deposited Joe's fastball into the street behind center field in the first game. Hopefully, the Generals' coaches had signaled an off-speed or breaking ball this time. I was wrong! Jose threw a fastball over the inner third of the plate. We all heard the crack of the bat and watched the ball sail over the fence once again. Tie game.

Both pitchers settled in and threw flawlessly over the next several innings. Jose had pitched magnificently through five innings except for giving up the bomb in the first inning. His fastball velocity was 92-93 mph and stayed on the outer third of the plate while the slider had late break. He occasionally mixed in changeups to keep the free-swinging Pelicans off balance at the plate. Jose had caught the attention of the crowd of college and professional scouts and they watched intently. Perhaps Jose could parlay his performance on the NCT big stage into a college scholarship offer or a free-agent contract with a professional team.

In the sixth inning Jose's fastball velocity dropped to the 88-89 mph range and was more hittable. At the lower velocity, his fastballs had to be fine and just touch the edge of the plate to avoid turning the game into batting practice for the Pelicans. To make matters worse, the umpire's strike zone appeared to get smaller as the game progressed. The Pelicans' first two batters flew out on line drives to the outfield. Jose then walked the next two batters due to the postage stamp strike zone being called by the home plate umpire. Unable to stay on the edges of the plate with his fastball, Jose relied exclusively on breaking balls to get out of the inning. He was exhausted as he walked to the dugout after getting the final out of the sixth inning. We entered the last inning still tied 1-1. Mike Rizzo and the coaches had to make a pitching decision while the Generals batted. Did Jose have enough in the tank to pitch another inning or would the coaches have to look to another arm in the bullpen?

The bottom of our lineup was up to bat at the top of the last inning. Catcher Brock Dillard would lead off the inning followed by third baseman Owen Sorensen. On the first pitch, Brock hit a soft flyball to the right fielder who caught it for the first out. Sorensen took his first pitch for a ball and then doubled on a line drive down the right field line. Joe settled into the batter's box. The Pelicans' pitching coach walked to the mound for a visit and signaled the infield to play up on the grass in anticipation of a bunt. The first pitch was a breaking ball in the dirt. The next pitch was a high fastball. Joe faked a bunt and then slashed a Texas Leaguer to right field for a base hit. The Generals had runners on the corners and Alberts would bat next.

This was an ideal situation for the Generals as Alberts had a very hot bat. The first pitch was a called strike on the inside corner. Then Alberts turned on a changeup and hit the ball down the third base line. It was a sizzling line drive. The third baseman dived towards the bag and made a fantastic catch. Sorensen had taken a three-step leadoff and could not get back to the bag before the third baseman touched the bag to execute an unassisted double play. The Pelicans had avoided giving up a run and now would be up to bat.

We looked with anticipation towards the field wondering which General would be on the mound for the final inning of the game. Then Josh took the hill. He was going to try to close two consecutive championship games. He had only thrown 20 pitches in the first championship game so hopefully he could get it done now.

The first pitch was a fastball that hit the batter in the knee. It was a painful injury and the batter took his time limping down to first base. The second batter executed a perfectly placed sacrifice bunt that advanced the runner to second base. The next two batters struck out but the Pelican base runner had managed to advance to third base on a wild pitch by Josh.

The Pelicans were down to their last out. Mike Rizzo called a timeout and slowly walked to the mound for a conference with Josh. The speedy Pelican center fielder was up to bat. What would be the strategy? Rizzo left the mound and walked back to the dugout. There was no defensive shift and the infielders played at the normal depth.

The first pitch was a 97-mph fastball that the Pelican center fielder swung at and missed. Josh rocked back on the mound and fired his second pitch, another fastball, towards the plate. The batter surprised everyone and bunted the ball towards third base. The runner had broken early and would get safely to home plate. The only question was if Josh could field the ball quickly enough and throw the batter out at first.

The batter exploded out of the box and sprinted

to first base while Josh broke to field the bunt. Josh picked up the ball and spun to throw it in one smooth motion. The ball hit the first baseman's glove at the exact moment the runner touched the base. The batter was safe and the run scored. The game was over and the East Cobb Pelicans were NCT champions this summer.

● ● ●

Now that the season was over I knew there was one unpleasant task ahead of me. I walked over to the boys as they stood in line to board the team bus back to the hotel.

"Would you guys like to ride with me in the rental car? We could stop for a snack. There are some things I'd like to discuss with you."

"Sure, sounds good," said Josh as we walked to the middle of the parking lot.

I opened the trunk of the rental car so the boys could load their baseball bags. Josh and Joe got in the back seat while Mark sat next to me in front. Then we started to navigate through the streets congested with game traffic to make our way to the Pima Freeway for the short ride to the hotel.

"What did you want to talk about?" said Joe.

"Well, I mostly want to talk to Mark but you and Josh are his friends so you should hear this too," I said.

Mark looked over at me and said, "Mr. Jones, what's going on?"

"Mark, your dad came out to Arizona to watch you play."

"Was he at the game tonight?"

"I don't think he was here today but he did see

the game last night," I said.

Mark grimaced. "Will I get to see him?"

"I don't think so. He came to my room late last night but then left with two men."

Mark had a worried expression on his face and asked, "Is Dad in trouble?"

"I'm not sure what happened after they left my room but I do know the two men wanted your dad to give them some money," I said. "The police are looking for your dad and the men."

Joe and Josh exchanged glances in the back seat but didn't say anything. Mark sat expressionless and said nothing.

"Mark, I called your aunt and uncle. They're going to meet us at the airport in Dallas tomorrow morning."

After a few more minutes, we were finally on the Pima Freeway and making good time. Mark looked at me again and asked, "Would it be all right if you just dropped me off at the hotel? I'm not really hungry."

"Yeah, I'm not hungry either," said Josh.

We arrived back at the hotel and I dropped the boys off in front by the lobby before I returned the rental car.

CHAPTER 34

After I returned to my room in the hotel, I called Detective Truex to brief him on the events of the previous night. I was still a little upset that he had asked Maggie out after she provided him her thoughts on the lack of accounting controls at Tropical Investments. Truex picked up his phone after the third ring. Before he could say anything, I started the conversation,

"Truex, you're a horse's ass, I thought we were good friends and then you asked Maggie out on a date. What is that all about? I expected more from you, Vince."

"Lonny, please, don't take this too seriously, I was just kidding around with her."

"Yeah, sure you were... Well, I wanted to give you an update on Jack Heygood which could impact your investigation of Wendy Heygood's murder."

"I was hoping you'd call. The Phoenix Police called me earlier this morning to brief me on the events at your hotel."

"Jack Heygood came to my room in the middle of the night and was later kidnapped by a couple of thugs that were working for unhappy Tropical investors. Before he was abducted we had a chance to talk and he said the two men pursuing him were probably responsible for Wendy's death."

"Why did he think this was the case?" asked Truex.

"Jack said the two men told him they were coming to his home to collect money in the afternoon when Wendy was murdered. Jack fled the house when Wendy wouldn't give him any money to pay off the thugs and didn't warn her. She was a sitting duck when they arrived."

"Interesting, just as I thought, it was all about the Heygoods having large amounts of money that we couldn't explain."

"Well, I did get some insight on that," I said.

"Did he steal from Tropical Investments?"

"Maggie was spot on. Jack just laughed and confirmed what he did."

"Well, I still haven't been able to find any evidence to link Steve or Sara Sorensen directly to the murder so this information is probably my best lead. I'll follow up with the Phoenix Police to see if they turned up anything on Jack."

"Are you close to wrapping up the investigation?" I asked.

"Probably. This is the best information we've learned so far and there are really no other hot leads. Everything points to the two thugs that abducted Heygood and there certainly was a motive. I wanted to talk to Jack Heygood, especially after learning about his tawdry affair during my trip to

Palm Beach, but that seems unlikely now after his abduction. I'm sure the chief would like to put this murder case to bed. If we obtain more information and locate the two thugs then we may reopen the case but that's probably not going to happen. By the way, how is your trip to Phoenix going?" added Vince.

"The Generals had a fantastic tournament but lost in the championship to a team from East Cobb, Georgia."

"Yes, the game came down to the final out."

"How did you know that?"

"I watched all of your games on web TV," said Vince, laughing.

"I guess I was wrong about you, Vince. You are a baseball guy!"

The next morning my wake-up call from the front desk came at 5:00. I had done most of my packing the previous night so I threw on some clothes, grabbed my suitcase and headed to the lobby. Most of the players and parents had already assembled in the lobby as our bus to the airport was scheduled to leave shortly. I glanced out the main entrance to the circular driveway in front of the hotel and caught a glimpse of Butch and Nick piling into the red Corvette for the long drive back to Lubbock. The airport bus arrived ten minutes later and the Generals hurried to the airport to catch the 7:00 National Airlines flight back to Dallas. Even though we lost, the tournament had been a great experience for the boys. Hopefully, the nucleus of the team would return next summer and the Generals could make another run at the NCT.

I texted Maggie just before we boarded our flight: "Hi Maggie, we're at the airport on our way home, I can't wait to see you."

A few seconds later Maggie's return text arrived: "Look forward to seeing you Lonny, I want to talk."

CHAPTER 35

The flight back to DFW arrived on time and we took the DART train to the station where I had parked my Mustang GT. The day was beautiful with only a few clouds in the sky and the temperature was still below 90 degrees so we drove home with the windows down. Mark Heygood's aunt picked him up at DFW so only Joe and Josh were in the car with me.

"The tournament was fun but it sure feels good to be home," said Joe.

"I'm going to hang around for a couple of days before I take 'The Dog' back to Lubbock," said Josh.

We rounded the corner and headed up the street to the house. I slowed down as we passed by Maggie's house; a crew of painters applied a fresh coat of white paint to the exterior, and all of the trees and shrubs in her yard looked like they had been recently trimmed.

The boys looked over too and Josh said,

"Maggie's house looks pretty sharp."

We continued down the street to my house and I parked in the driveway in front of the house so we could easily unload. We emptied the car in five minutes. I thought about just walking down to Maggie's house but decided to call first. The phone rang several times before Maggie answered, "Hi Lonny, are you back in Dallas?"

"We're at the house. I thought about coming over, but with all of the activity there, is now a good time?" I asked.

There was a brief silence and then Maggie said, "Ah...sure, now is good."

Maggie sounded a little different but I was anxious to see her and started walking down the street. Her house hadn't looked this good in years; the new glossy white paint was a definite improvement and the lawn and shrubs looked carefully manicured. I dodged the wet paint signs and went in the front door. There was Maggie greeting me with a hug. "Let's go in the living room and talk."

We walked hand in hand and sat on the couch with a good view of the front yard.

"How was your trip to Arizona?" she asked.

"We made a good run but came in second to East Cobb."

"Did Joe have a good tournament?"

"Yes, I think so; he batted well and the scouts complimented him on his pitching."

Maggie and I just looked at each other as an awkward silence passed between us. I glanced out of the window and said, "The outside of your house looks great, why did you decide to make these improvements?"

The smile left Maggie's face and she locked eyes with mine. "There is something I need to tell you."

"What is it?" I asked.

"I was offered the District VP job in Houston on a full-time basis and...I accepted."

I started breathing hard, my body felt numb and I was dizzy. Another long, awkward silence passed while I looked at Maggie in disbelief.

Maggie looked at me with a concerned look on her face, "Lonny, are you okay? You don't look well."

My head was spinning and I was speechless. I was totally devastated. Just then a truck with a Flaw Realty sign on the side pulled up in front of the house. Two men got out of the truck. The driver picked up a shovel from the back of the truck while the passenger unloaded a flashy red "For Sale by Flaw Realty" sign.

I looked at Maggie, pointed at the men and sarcastically said, "At least I didn't find out you were leaving by seeing the sign."

My head throbbed and my whole body hurt. I was angry and close to screaming but all the energy had been drained from my body. I had no air in my lungs.

"Lonny, I'm sorry you had to find out this way," said Maggie with a pained look on her face.

"Now I get it, you had already decided you were leaving before the trip to Phoenix, that is why Jim Flaw was over here," I said.

"Well...I...really...it was very hard—"

"That's bullshit. I expected a lot more from you, Maggie." I stood up but my knees felt weak and the room was spinning.

Her face turned red. "I wanted to tell you sooner but you were in Arizona."

"For God's sake, you have my telephone number."

Maggie remained seated but said nothing. I needed to get out of her house before I said something that I might really regret. As I started walking out, Maggie started to cry. "I'm doing this to be with my daughters and grandson—they need me."

I stopped and slowly turned to look at Maggie directly in the eyes. "Well, Maggie, what about me?"

There was nothing left to be said so I walked out the front door. The Flaw Realty guys were almost done setting up the "For Sale" sign in the front yard a few feet from the curb. I quickly walked home and grabbed a cold, 16-ounce Coors from the refrigerator before I went outside to sit at my patio table. My head was spinning like I was going to pass out so I leaned over and put my head directly on the table. I couldn't move for several minutes. Then the phone rang; it was Maggie. As far as I was concerned, it was over so I just let it ring.

CHAPTER 36

My last meeting of the day at National Airlines ended at 7:30 p.m. The workdays had been extended since my financial analysis team was now deployed on a secret acquisition study in addition to our regular duties. National Airlines constantly evaluated potential merger and acquisition targets. One particular opportunity, Global Airways, had attracted interest from senior management. Recently, the pace of the evaluation had increased and was now a secret project with code name "Green Field." Usually a strategic project like this begins with the Corporate Development group and expands into a cross-department team if more than a cursory analysis is required. Since my team did financial analysis in addition to analytics, we were asked to participate.

My immediate objective was to estimate the value of the Global Airways takeoff and landing slots at John F. Kennedy Airport in New York City and

Dulles International Airport in Washington. The work on the Green Field project had an aggressive completion date so I was putting in 60-hour weeks and spending very little time at the house with Joe.

I could hardly wait to get out of the headquarters building and quickly walked to the garage to get to my car for the short trip home. The drive was uneventful and traffic moved at a fast pace since rush hour was over. As I drove up my street I noticed Jim Flaw standing by the sale sign in Maggie's front yard. I pulled over and rolled the front passenger window down so we could talk.

"Hi Jim, what's with the house?"

"We have a buyer and hope to close in a couple of weeks," said Jim as he attached a "Contract Pending" sign.

"I'm sure Maggie will be happy when the sale closes," I said.

"I talked to her today. She plans to live with her daughter on the west side of Houston before she buys," said Jim.

"Good for her."

"She did ask about you. I told her that I don't see you around the street very often."

"Say hello when you talk to her next. Things have heated up at work so I'm not at the house as much."

My conversation with Jim ended and I pulled into my driveway as Joe and his free-spirit girlfriend, Ann, were leaving the house. We met halfway up the driveway.

"Hi guys, are you hungry? Burgers on the grill?" I asked.

"Ann and I are headed out to a party and we might go over to the Heygoods' house to swim later," said Joe.

"I'm glad you two are enjoying the last few weeks of summer vacation. Be careful at the Heygoods', I heard the new owner plans to move in soon."

Joe and Ann continued walking down the driveway hand in hand toward his ten-year-old Honda Accord parked on the street. I didn't quiz Joe about what he and Ann do together at the house every day but I think he's into something good. Since it was just myself, I didn't want to grill so I decided to zap the barbeque leftovers from last night. The spicy sausage wasn't half bad and I washed it down with a large glass of milk. The only thing interesting on TV was an NFL exhibition game from Mexico City. I checked the clock during a timeout in the fourth quarter. It was almost midnight. I decided to shower and go to bed since tomorrow was going to be another long day.

I woke up at 2:00 a.m. and looked for Joe in the house but there was no sign of him. He didn't answer his cell phone so it was time to go out and look for him. The first stop would be the Heygoods' house. I threw some clothes on and jumped into the Mustang for the ten-minute ride. The Heygoods' house looked completely black inside as I approached it on Strait Lane and there appeared to be no outside lights on. Joe had told me that Ann liked to go skinny-dipping so I wanted to see what was going on in the pool as discretely as possible. I remained in the shadows as I quietly walked around the house towards the swimming pool in the backyard. I peered around the corner and saw there was no activity in the pool but I did notice some movement about eighty feet away. There appeared to be three men digging a hole. It was too dark to see much of anything; I could just see their silhouettes. Behind them I could see some sort of vehicle parked in back. This seemed very strange so I decided to call Lieutenant Truex.

Vince's cell phone rang ten times before he finally answered. "Truex here."

"Vince, this is Lonny and I am looking for Joe. I'm at the Heygoods' house."

"Jesus Christ, it's three o'clock in the morning. Why are you calling me?"

"Vince, Joe is not here but I stumbled onto three men in the backyard digging a hole."

"Did they see you?"

"No, I stayed in the shadows near the house and close to the shrubs."

"Meet me in front of the house," said Vince. "I'll be there in fifteen minutes."

From a distance I could see the men continue to dig but was too far away to hear anything they were saying. After fifteen minutes I quietly walked to the front of the house. Vince had already arrived and was carrying a large flashlight.

"Here's what we are going to do—you stay out of sight near the house when I get their attention," said Vince.

"That works," I said.

We started to walk around the south side of the Heygoods' house. Just before we reached the backyard Vince turned to me. "Are you carrying?"

I shook my head. "Nope, I left my pistol at home."

Vince removed his backup Glock 27 pistol from his rear holster and handed it to me. He laughed and said, "Keep this just in case I get in a shootout.

You've got fifteen bullets."

I crouched out of view by the side of the house as Vince turned the corner, pointed his flashlight at the three men and said, "This is the Dallas Police, stay where you are."

Immediately the men dropped their shovels and there was a short moment of silence. Then I could see the flashes of their guns and heard "bang, bang, bang" as bullets started flying through the air. Truex hit the deck and tried to get small as the men continued to fire. Bullets were landing in the ground close to him. Dirt was flying and I could smell gunpowder in the air. I assumed a shooter's stance partially protected by the corner of the house and aimed the Glock 27. Then I rapidly fired four shots at the three men. They were surprised and ducked down for a moment that gave Truex a few seconds to reposition himself behind a thick tree and return fire with his Glock 22.

The gun battle continued. Bullets ricocheted off the bricks of the Heygoods' house to my left. One of the men retrieved something about the size of a small suitcase from the hole as the other two continued to fire. Then the three men started to retreat towards the vehicle as I continued to fire the Glock 27. One of them grabbed his leg and briefly fell to the ground. Soon the three men jumped into the vehicle behind them and rapidly drove away. The shooting only lasted five minutes but it seemed like an eternity.

Detective Truex and I slowly walked towards the hole with our guns drawn. The hole was empty and the surrounding ground was littered with shell casings. An unopened pack of Marlboro cigarettes was on the ground to the right of the hole. Truex carefully picked up the cigarette package and said, "We need to dust this for fingerprints."

"A package of Marlboros fell out of Jack Heygood's pocket in my room in Arizona," I said.

"Interesting coincidence, maybe the lab boys can provide some insight," said Detective Truex.

In less than five minutes two police cars arrived and the officers jumped out with their guns drawn. "Guys, you are a little late, the war ended ten minutes ago," said Truex laughing.

Detective Truex and I were immediately driven downtown to file a report. A sergeant took our statements at a small table at the front of the office area. Once our statements were complete, the sergeant walked them into the captain's office. After twenty minutes, the captain emerged from his office and walked directly towards us with a frown on his face.

"I want you guys in my office now," said the captain as he turned towards his office.

We followed him in and a sergeant shut the door behind us. All three of us remained standing.

"Truex, what were you thinking?" said the captain. He scowled. "You and a citizen have a gun battle with three people digging a hole in the backyard of a home in North Dallas."

"Sir, we tried to contain the shooting as much as possible," said Truex.

"Neighbors reported hearing over fifty shots fired. Do you call that containing the shooting?" said the captain.

Vince and I exchanged glances but said nothing.

"Why didn't you wait and call in SWAT?" continued the captain.

"I thought they were just three punks

vandalizing the backyard," said Truex.

The captain's face turned red and he frowned.

"Well, you guessed wrong," said the captain.

A frown appeared on Truex's face. "I identified myself and the three men immediately started firing at me. I had no idea they were armed to the teeth and would shoot."

"Police watchdog groups are going to be all over me and the department. All I have to show is a detective, a citizen, a hole in the ground and bullet holes in several surrounding homes in an upscale North Dallas neighborhood," said the captain. "We're lucky nobody was killed."

The captain looked down at the report and shook his head. "Truex, do you normally let citizens get involved in shootings?"

"I was pinned down by three shooters," said Truex. "I had no way out so Lonny backed me up."

The captain rolled his eyes, looked at me and asked, "Mr. Jones, do you even know how to use a gun?"

Before I could say anything, Detective Truex intervened. "Jones is a Hollywood Marine and knows how to shoot."

The captain looked at me for a few seconds and smiled. "San Diego is a cake walk; real Marines go through Paris Island."

I looked at the captain and nodded with a small grin on my face but didn't say anything.

"Well, Mr. Jones, what do you have to say?" asked the captain.

"There was a lot of lead flying through the air; they had Truex pinned down on the grass," I said.

"So why were you in Heygoods' backyard?"

"Joe, my son, told me his girlfriend wanted to go

skinny-dipping in the Heygoods' pool. He didn't come home tonight so I went out to look for him and the Heygoods' house was my first stop."

The captain shook his head in disbelief. "Could you identify any of the three men you saw digging the hole?"

"No, not really, it was too dark. All of the lights in the back of the house and near the pool had been turned off."

Another officer entered the room and handed a piece of paper to the captain who stopped talking and started reading the paper. "The lab dusted the Marlboro package but we didn't find any of Heygood's fingerprints," said the captain.

"Maybe they were all wearing gloves when they dug the hole," speculated Truex.

The captain sat silent for a minute, leaned back and looked at Truex and me. "I thought we put this Heygood murder investigation to bed after Jack was abducted in Arizona. I don't want to open it up again unless we have some solid evidence. I think what we have here is a case of three armed burglars who were interrupted in the course of a felony," said the captain. He stood up and walked around his desk. "Mr. Jones, thank you for your time and I hope you find your son," said the captain as he shook my hand. "Internal Affairs may call you to ask some follow-up questions."

Detective Truex glanced at me and frowned at the captain's last comment. It was 4:30 a.m. and time to get home. Vince walked me down to my car.

"Something doesn't smell right about the hole in the backyard. This is not a routine burglary," said Vince.

"I have to agree with you," I remarked. "I feel

Jack Heygood is somehow involved."

"Well you never saw him get killed by the two thugs. So anything is possible. He could still be alive," said Vince. "I didn't get a good look at the shooters but two of them looked pretty big. I wonder if they were the guys who abducted Jack from my hotel room in Arizona."

I shook Vince's hand and then jumped in the Mustang for the ride home. The drive from police headquarters to my neighborhood took only twenty minutes since the morning rush would start in an hour. When I drove up my street towards the house I spotted Joe's Accord parked as usual next to the curb in front.

CHAPTER 37

Project Green Field continued to move along as scheduled for the next month at National Airlines. The expanding analysis showed that the synergies gained by combining the assets of both companies had tremendous economic value but that the training costs associated with merging the pilot seniority lists and bringing the Global Airways aircraft up to National Airlines maintenance standards would be prohibitive. Rumors spread that there were other potential suitors and so there was a heightened sense of urgency to close a deal.

I sat in my office with Skip Wise, VP of Corporate Development, drinking a cup of coffee and talking about Project Green Field when his cell phone started ringing. He picked it up and his facial muscles tightened.

"They want me upstairs in the weekly planning meeting now. This is probably about Green Field. You're coming with me," Skip said.

We grabbed some notepads. "I hate just getting called up to the planning meeting without any warning. Usually, they don't call you up to thank you or slap you on the back," I joked.

Skip turned to me and said, "If things go bad up there, don't start yelling. We'll put it back together later."

It was a short walk to the elevator bank and we jumped into the next elevator going up. The seventh floor housed the executive offices and conference rooms. We walked into the CEO's large conference room and all of the senior executives were seated around a circular table. There were whiteboards on all of the walls and coffee was brewing on a table to the right of the double doors. CEO William "Bill" Wolf and President Daniel "Dan" McAfferty were seated next to each near the doors. Bill Wolf looked like a Cheshire cat with his large glistening teeth. Dan McAfferty had gray hair and was drinking from a large cup of coffee. Skip and I stood at the far end of the room directly across the table from Bill and Dan. Some of the seated senior leaders looked at us and laughed because they knew we were in the hot seat.

Bill Wolf looked at the group and began to speak. "First and foremost, we need to get Green Field moving. Northern Airlines is going to make a bid. We can't let them beat us to the table."

Dan McAfferty, with a cigarette in his hand, paused for a moment and said in a low voice, "Bill, you're absolutely right. I want to see some real focus. We need to engage with Global within the next week."

I glanced at Bill Wolf. He had a very intense look on his face. I thought he was going to scream.

The room became silent and everyone had their game face on.

Bill grimaced and then started to speak with a raised voice as he pounded the table with his fist. "Gents, we need to get this done. Northern is trying to steal food from our table. We need to crush them. I want Global's East Coast slots and routes to England."

Dan McAfferty scowled at the seated executives and said, "We are going to kick Northern's ass. I don't want the deal to include Global's pilots or aircraft, just slots and routes." Then Dan stood and pointed directly at Skip and me with his right index finger. "Skip, get it done!"

Skip and I looked at Bill Wolf and Dan McAfferty for a few seconds and nodded our heads. The message had been communicated and it was time for us to leave. We headed to the elevators and back to Skip's office to discuss our next moves.

• • •

We had determined that this acquisition would provide much more value to us than to any of our competitors including Northern Airlines but we also thought they might act to prevent our getting the upper hand in several regions of the country. Senior management contacted Global Airways through a trusted back channel and informed them of our interest. Global Airways, headquartered in a suburb of New York City, seemed to be very interested in our overtures and was willing to meet. We needed to select a site for these discussions and immediately ruled out Dallas and New York. I preferred Chicago as it would be in another competitor's backyard. An early snowstorm had already shut down the Northeast so I was not surprised that Global Airways pushed for a meeting in Florida.

"Do these guys want to talk or play golf?" I asked.

"Those guys are looking at twelve inches of snow tonight so I can't blame them," said Skip.

Several sites in Florida were considered but we eventually settled on Fort Lauderdale since both companies had direct flights to the city from their headquarters.

CHAPTER 38

The National Airlines 7:30 p.m. departure to Fort Lauderdale landed on time and the negotiating team boarded a shuttle bus to the hotel. The negotiations were going to be held at a plush resort with a 36-hole golf course. Skip Wise's cell phone started ringing and he quickly picked up and listened for thirty seconds. Then he hung up, turned to us and said, "Global's team won't arrive until late tomorrow night so we need to push the meeting back. You guys have tomorrow off, so get out on the links."

This was my first trip to this part of Florida so I picked up a rental car the next morning after eating breakfast and started driving north on Highway 1 to see the sights. I passed through Pompano Beach and pulled into a convenience store in Boca Raton to get a drink. Detective Truex had volunteered to check in on Joe while I was in Florida so I thought I better give him a call to find out how last night worked out. Since Joe knew a policeman was going to be coming to the house I thought he would be less likely to do something stupid. I called Vince's cell phone and he answered after the first ring. "Truex here."

"Hi Vince, it's beautiful down here. We have the day off and I am sightseeing in Boca Raton. Did you have a chance to go to the house and visit Joe?"

"Well...I went over last night after your neighbors called the police," said Vince.

I was startled and spilled some of the drink on my shirt. "What? Neighbors called the police?"

"The party was getting loud and there was drinking in the front yard. There was one keg in the house and another in the backyard," said Vince.

I shook my head. "Party? Drinking in the front yard? I don't believe it."

"Lonny, one other thing, there was some breakage inside but a handyman like you could repair it in a couple of weeks."

"I knew Joe wasn't ready to stay by himself. What was I thinking?"

"I shut the party down and had a long talk with Joe," said Vince. "I told him that he would be staying with me if the police were called again."

"Okay, thanks Vince, I should be back in a couple of days. Please keep an eye on Joe."

"No problem. So you're in Boca Raton, that's pretty close to where I saw Jack's girlfriend in Delray Beach," said Vince.

I glanced at the map and said, "Delray is just north of Boca Raton. Wasn't her name Sunny?"

"Yes, that's her nickname. Her real name is Angelica Austin," said Vince.

"Okay, now I remember, bleached-blond hair, a figure that doesn't quit and a big tattoo on her back," I said.

"You know, I never got into Sunny's apartment. I didn't have enough evidence to go to the local police and try to get a search warrant. If Jack Heygood is alive, I bet there's some scrap of information in there that could help find him," said Vince.

"You talked with Sunny, right?" I asked.

"She works at a biker bar off the main highway called The Beachcomber. It's right on the water," said Vince. "Her apartment is just across the street."

"Okay, got it."

"Lonny, I want to make one thing clear, I am not recommending or condoning illegal activities to obtain evidence."

"I know," I said. "You are only here to protect and serve."

Vince laughed. "You can't miss Sunny if she still works at The Beachcomber."

There was a brief pause. "Lonny, one other thing. I got a call from Maggie—she wants to talk to you. I think she realizes she made a big mistake moving to Houston," said Vince. "I know you went through a tough period after she left, but Maggie is a good woman."

"I'm not ready to call her. Why can't she just pick up the phone and call me?" I asked.

"She thinks you are still angry since she didn't give you any warning that she was moving."

"That hurt me bad. Real bad." I paused for a moment and continued, "Yeah, she needs to call me."

"Okay Lonny, I will look in on Joe every day until you get back. Be safe," said Vince before he hung up the phone.

CHAPTER 39

Northbound traffic was stop-and-go on S. Federal Highway but thirty minutes later I pulled into The Beachcomber's parking lot in Delray Beach. A beach with beautiful white sand was on the east side of The Beachcomber. The water was light blue and small waves were visible in the distance. I walked across the parking lot to the main entrance. There were probably twenty motorcycles in the lot and ten to twelve cars.

The Beachcomber had a large circular bar and several fish mounted on the wall, just as Vince had described it. Several bikers were sitting at the bar wearing their leather jackets and cutting up. It looked like a pretty rough crowd. There were a few empty stools at the other end of the bar from the bikers so I walked around the bar and sat down. I glanced at the insignia on the leather jackets—this was not a local motorcycle club. These guys were members of a notorious, nationwide motorcycle gang.

My eyes scanned the inside of The Beachcomber from left to right. The only waitress at the bar had red hair and was flirting with the bikers. A marlin mounted on the wall to my right caught my attention when suddenly I heard someone say, "What can I get for you, honey?"

I quickly turned to my left and saw a curvaceous blonde waitress with beautiful blue eyes and immediately understood why Jack Heygood risked his marriage to be with her. Sunny had very soft features and was one of the best-looking women I had ever seen. Her large, shapely breasts screamed for attention. I took a deep breath and just gazed at her. Sunny looked at me and smiled as if she was used to that kind of reaction from first-time bar patrons. After a few more seconds, I collect my thoughts and said, "May I have a Coors Banquet?"

Sunny cocked her head to the side. "Sure, would you like a shot of whisky with that?"

I laughed. "No, just the beer, thanks."

She smiled and walked over to the tap to pour my beer. I glanced over at the bikers and several of them appeared to be studying her figure.

In a couple of minutes Sunny was back with my beer and leaned on the bar with her right side towards me. Her right breast was almost touching the bar. She noticed my gazes and laughed.

"Is this your first time at The Beachcomber?"

"Yes it is; I am just in town for a convention."

"Well thanks for coming, my name is Sunny."

"Pleasure to meet you, I'm Jimmy Woodcock," I responded. It wasn't a very good name but it was all I could come up with at the time.

"Jimmy, what line of work are you in?"

"I do a little bit of this and a little bit of that but

mostly insurance."

"How long are you going to be in town?"

"I'll be here a few more days," I said.

Sunny leaned a little bit closer. "Has anyone ever told you that you have a Texas accent?"

"Yes, as a matter of fact, I live in San Antonio."

Sunny walked outside to service the tables facing the beach on the deck. In five minutes she was back in front of me leaning on the bar. She turned and looked at me for a few moments before saying, "Jimmy, tell me about you."

"The last year has been very rough; my wife and dog died in a car accident. They were hit by a drunk driver."

"Jimmy, that's terrible. I am so sorry," said Sunny with a concerned look. She put her right hand on my left hand and lightly squeezed.

"How long have you been working here at The Beachcomber?" I asked.

"My boyfriend and I moved down from West Palm two years ago after we got laid off."

"Your boyfriend?" I asked, hoping to get some information about Jack.

"Well, actually we have an open relationship. He is only here a couple of weeks every month so I get a chance to meet some interesting guys," said Sunny as she held my left hand with both of her hands and looked into my eyes.

I thought this might be the opportunity to get into Sunny's apartment. "Sunny, is there any way I can see you later tonight after work?"

"I was hoping you would ask. I get off work at midnight."

I smiled and squeezed her hand. "That's great."

"Just so you know, it's two hundred cash or

three hundred if you want to spend the night," said Sunny as she winked at me.

I gave her a knowing smile. "See you tonight."

I finished my beer and walked outside in the bright sunshine to my rental car.

CHAPTER 40

Vince's phone rang five times before he answered, "Truex."

"Vince, I have a date with Sunny at midnight. She basically confirmed that Jack is still alive."

"Wow, talk to me. How did you get the date with Sunny?" Vince asked.

"Sunny does tricks when Jack is out of town. I was an easy target."

"Tell me about Jack," said Vince.

"He is in town with Sunny only a couple of weeks a month; they have an open relationship."

"This is the break I've been waiting for. I'm going to take the next flight down to Florida," said Vince.

"You should be able to get here by ten tonight if you leave for the airport now."

Just then I got a beep that someone was calling me and I needed to answer. "Vince, I have to go, bring me a gun and call me when you get here," I said before I hung up and switched over to the other call.

"Jones here," I announced.

"Lonny, where the hell are you? The guys want to tee off at four to get in eighteen holes," said Skip.

"I've been playing tourist and checking things out. I won't be back to the hotel until much later. I'm going to have to pass," I said.

"C'mon Lonny, what are you doing?"

"Would you believe me if I told you I have been drinking in a biker bar and have a date with a hooker later?" I said.

"Jones, don't give me that bullshit. You need to be back here for our seven o'clock meeting with Global in the morning."

"Okay, catch you on the flip side," I said just before hanging up.

I had nine hours to kill before my date with Sunny so I decided to drive across the street and take a look at her apartment. The mailboxes were located in the middle of the complex on the ground floor and I saw that Austin was the name on the box for apartment #205. I walked up the stairs to the second floor and peered into the windows of the apartment. The living room was simply furnished with a table, couch and two chairs. The curtains to the other room were closed so I had no idea what was inside. I looked closely at the last window I checked; the bottom sliding pane was raised a little bit too high to be locked. An older couple appeared and passed by me so I started walking the other direction until they turned to walk down the hallway. Nobody was in sight so I walked back to the window and pulled it up. It was open so I lifted my leg and stepped over the windowsill into the apartment.

The room had a mattress on the floor and large mirrors on a couple of the walls. I thought this must be the room where Sunny entertains her customers. I continued down the hall and went in the master bedroom. There was a travel bag on the floor filled with dirty clothes and a leather toiletry kit with the initials JH on it. I wondered if Jack was back in town. The hallway continued into the kitchen and there was an open can of beer on the counter—it was still colder than room temperature. Someone had recently been in the apartment.

Then I heard a key in the door. I retreated back into the room with the open window and shut the door as I found it. I could hear steps in the hallway and then the radio went on in the bathroom closely followed by the sound of the shower. This was my opportunity to exit so I lifted the window, stepped outside and then shut it. I quickly walked down the steps to the first floor and then to my rental car.

I called Detective Truex's cell phone. The phone rang once and Vince answered.

"Lonny, what's up? We're getting ready to take off and the flight attendant is telling me to turn off my phone."

"Jack is here in Delray Beach. I just missed him in the apartment."

"Great, don't try to make any moves until I get there. I will call the local police once we take off," said Vince. "See you later."

I decided to park in the far corner of the lot in a space that provided a view to the front of apartment #205 so I could monitor any activities. I remained in position for several hours and finally the sun started to set. About 10:00 p.m. someone emerged from the apartment wearing a hoodie. It was too dark to make a positive identification as the person walked with a limp through the parking lot towards The Beachcomber but the height was about right; I thought it had to be Jack. Soon the person had crossed the highway and entered The Beachcomber. Twenty minutes passed and I spotted a person with a hoodie walking back towards the apartment. I wanted to tackle him but I thought better of it and decided to wait for Vince as ordered. Then I saw him open the door to a Ford truck, start the engine and drive away. This was an unexpected turn of events. An hour passed and there was no activity in the parking lot. I looked at my watch and it was a quarter to twelve, fifteen minutes before I was supposed to meet Sunny at The Beachcomber. Then my phone rang. It was Vince.

"Vince, where the hell are you?" I asked.

"I'm off behind the trees to your right with five Delray Beach policemen," said Vince.

"Jack was here a couple of hours ago but left in a Ford pickup. What do you want me to do?"

"Go to The Beachcomber to get Sunny and let her bring you back to the apartment. We will wait for Jack to return," Vince instructed.

I got out of the rental car and started walking across the street to The Beachcomber. There were only a few cars still in the lot and most of the motorcycles were gone. I walked through the front door and into the bar area. Sunny stood at the cash register closing out a tab. She turned to me and said, "Hi Jimmy, let me get my jacket and we can leave."

Soon we were walking out the front door and she grabbed my hand. "Jimmy, I have been thinking about you all day. Are you ready for a good time?"

I put my arm around her and we walked across the highway. Sunny stopped and held both of my hands. "I'm sorry there has been a change in plans. We need to make it a quickie. You can't stay the night."

"Why not?" I asked.

"My boyfriend is back in town and had to run an errand; he will be back around two am," said Sunny. "Will two hours be enough time for you or should we do this on another night?"

I hugged her and kissed her neck. "Sunny, you are a very beautiful woman; I want to make love to you now."

"Well let's go, what are we waiting for?" said Sunny with a big smile on her face. "Oh, by the way, do you have two hundred in cash?"

"Absolutely, I am ready to pay for services rendered," I said with a laugh.

I had taken this escapade with Sunny about as far as I wanted. Hopefully, Jack would return soon and be quickly apprehended by Truex and the Delray Beach Police.

We walked up the stairs to the apartment and Sunny reached in her purse for the key. Soon the door was open and we walked into the living room. I stopped and looked around as Sunny grabbed my shirt and said, "Not here. Let's take a shower together first and then go party."

Sunny started to walk down the hall and then turned and motioned me with her finger to follow.

"C'mon, Jimmy. It's going to be fun. Don't be nervous."

Sunny stepped towards me, grabbed my hand and led me to the bathroom. She turned to face me and then lifted her shirt over her head revealing her large and shapely breasts. With a big smile, she removed her short skirt. Sunny was completely naked except for her G-string.

Where was Truex? Where were the Delray Beach Police?

Sunny put her arms around my neck and kissed me softly. In seconds, she unbuttoned my shirt and tugged at my pants.

I glanced up at the sound of something coming from the hallway. The bathroom door flew open and I was face to face with Jack Heygood. Jack's face turned white when he saw Sunny and me standing almost naked together.

"Lonny, what the hell are you doing here?"

Sunny's jaw dropped. "Who the hell is Lonny?"

"Jack, Detective Truex is outside and wants to talk to you about Phoenix and the shooting in your backyard."

Jack looked horrified and immediately ran limping down the hallway into the back room and shut the door with a loud bang. Sunny, wearing only her G-string, ran down the hall after Jack and pounded on the closed door. "Jack, Jack, what's going on?"

Within seconds Vince and the five Delray Beach Police officers were in the apartment. The door to the back room was locked but the police broke it down in thirty seconds and then stormed the room with their guns drawn but Jack was gone—he had fled through a back window. It was fifteen feet straight down to the deck around the pool. We ran out the front door and looked down on the parking lot. Then we heard tires screeching as a Ford pickup flew off and disappeared on the highway heading north.

The first Delray Beach Police car was soon in pursuit with its lights flashing and siren blaring. A second police car pulled up at the bottom of the stairs and picked Vince and me up. I put on the rest of my clothes in the squad car as we headed north at a high rate of speed. Several minutes passed and then I heard a police operator say over the radio, "Suspect in Ford truck headed west on Boynton Beach Boulevard."

In a minute we reached Boynton Beach Boulevard and turned west. Soon we could see the first police car in the distance with its lights on approaching I95. I looked again thirty seconds later and it appeared that the police car had stopped. As we approached I95 we could see that all of the westbound traffic had stopped. Our driver steered the car over the median and we drove westbound in the eastbound lane. Just as we reached I95 we could see the Ford truck driving down the sidewalk trying to avoid the wreckage of a five-car collision in the I95 underpass. The first police car was stuck in the traffic and was blocked from going forward by a large firetruck. The Ford pickup drove a couple blocks down the street and then turned right onto NW 7th Street.

"How far north can he go on that street?" I asked.

One of the Boynton Beach policemen responded, "Only a few more blocks before he hits the Stanley Weaver Canal."

Jack was driving at least seventy miles per hour as he weaved through the residential neighborhood. The driver of our police car said, "He is reaching the end of NW 7th Street. He is going to have to turn left."

I saw Jack's brake lights as he made a hard left on the last street perpendicular to the canal. "We've got him. The street dead ends and there's a fence," said the officer driving the car.

Then the lights on Jack's truck bounced around as if he had gone off the road. One of the policemen announced over the radio, "Suspect drove through a fence and is in Pioneer Canal Park."

I looked at the Ford truck as it went around the park headed north and then disappeared again. We arrived at the park momentarily and went around the circular drive and looked out into the canal. The sky was clear and the stars were bright. Jack's truck was clearly visible in the water fifty feet from the end of a boat ramp. Jack had driven the truck down the ramp and into the canal. Only the top two feet of the cab were still visible as the truck was rapidly sinking.

"He was going so fast he probably didn't realize it was a boat ramp until it was too late to stop," Vince said.

One of the officers remarked, "There aren't any skid marks; he must have hit the water going fifty miles per hour."

In a few seconds we saw a figure waving his hands out of the window and then there was a thrashing sound in the water. We could hear Jack scream.

"What's going on?" I asked.

The policeman closest to me shook his head and shut his eyes. "This canal is full of alligators."

We paused and looked out towards the truck as it sank below the surface and the last of Jack's screams died out.

"They're going to have to get a boat out here and

look for the body," said Vince. "There is probably not much more that can be done tonight."

I looked at my watch and it was 2:30 a.m. "Could I get a ride to the apartment in Delray Beach? I need to drive my rental car back to Fort Lauderdale tonight," I said.

Thirty minutes later we reached Sunny's apartment complex across the highway from The Beachcomber. I got into the rental car and opened the windows. The cool sea breeze felt refreshing against my face. I backed the car out of the parking spot and then looked up towards apartment #205. All of the lights were on. Policemen walked in and out. I paused briefly before turning south on the highway and wondered what would become of Sunny. In a few minutes I was speeding down I95 towards my hotel in Fort Lauderdale with the windows down and the radio on.

CHAPTER 41

The sun was coming up when I pulled into the parking lot of the resort in Fort Lauderdale. We would begin negotiations with Global Airways in two hours and I needed to take a shower and lie down. The previous twenty-four hours had been a beatdown. I took the elevator up to my floor and walked into my room. The message light on my room phone was bright red so I called the voicemail and listened.

"Lonny, this is Skip Wise, your cell phone battery must be dead. Call me as soon as you get in."

I checked my cell phone; there were two calls from Skip a little after midnight. Skip's room was two doors down. I called his room directly using the hotel phone. The phone rang five times before Skip answered. "Hello..." he said in a groggy voice.

"Top of the morning, Skip."

"For God's sake, what time is it?"

"Probably about fifteen minutes before your

alarm goes off," I said.

"Why didn't you answer your phone last night?"

I laughed. "Would you believe me if I told you I was just about to get in the shower with a hooker when you called?"

"Lonny, your bullshit is getting kind of old," said Skip. "Here's the deal, our meeting is canceled; Northern Airlines is negotiating with Global right now in New York City."

"No wonder Global pushed our meeting back a day. How'd you find out?"

"Dan McAfferty called me and started screaming," Skip said. "He thinks we weren't aggressive enough about scheduling the meeting with Global."

"Well, Global is going to want to talk before they accept a Northern offer. We'll still get an opportunity."

"Pack your clothes; we're booked on the eight-fifteen flight back to Dallas," said Skip. "The airport shuttle leaves at six-thirty."

CHAPTER 42

Our flight was delayed departing Fort Lauderdale due to a brief thunderstorm so we landed an hour late at DFW. I turned on my phone as we taxied to the gate and it immediately started ringing. Vince was calling. "Hello Vince," I said.

"We found a suitcase with two hundred thousand dollars in Heygood's truck after we pulled it from the canal," said Vince.

"Wow, that's not too surprising," I said. "I guess it was always about the money."

"The divers recovered his left arm with lots of bite marks in the water near the truck but there was no sign of the rest of Jack's body."

"How do you know it was Jack's arm?" I asked.

"There's a small yellow tattoo of a sun on the forearm."

I gasped. "Jesus...I've seen the tattoo."

"Thanks for confirming the identity. We think the alligators got the rest of him. The Coast Guard is going to dredge this part of the canal to see what else we can come up with."

I shook my head. "That's terrible."

"Makes you wonder what Jack's relationship was with the two thugs that grabbed him in Arizona."

"Either the abduction was a complete hoax to get us off Jack's trail or he made them an offer they couldn't refuse after he was abducted," I speculated.

"Jack must have split the money with them; I thought we would have found more than two hundred thousand," said Vince.

"Thanks for the update," I said. "Give me a call when you get to back to Dallas."

The negotiating team deplaned and walked down to the lower level of the terminal to catch the airport shuttle for the short ride back to the National Airlines headquarters.

My head was killing me and I didn't have any appointments since I planned to be out of the office so I decided to leave early and go home to assess the damage from Joe's party and chew him out. The mid-afternoon traffic was light so I made good time back to Dallas. I turned the corner to drive up my street and passed Maggie's house. The "Contract Pending" sign had been replaced by a "Sold" sign. I shook my head, didn't slow down and kept on driving. Then I looked up the street to my house. Joe's Accord was parked on the street and a Jeep Cherokee sat in the driveway. I did a double take. That was Maggie's SUV!

CHAPTER 43

I pulled into my driveway and parked directly behind Maggie's Cherokee. This was certainly an unexpected development. I wondered why she was here and remained seated in the Mustang *Bullitt* for a few moments to collect my thoughts. As I exited the car I heard a sound and quickly looked to my left; Joe was waving and walking towards me.

"Hi Dad, good to see you," said Joe.

Frowning at Joe, I said, "We need to talk. I expected a lot more from you when I decided to let you stay alone at the house."

"Maggie came by thirty minutes ago and I invited her to come inside. I knew you would like that," said Joe.

"Joe, don't try to change the subject, you're in the dog house," I said. "Vince told me the neighbors called the police because of the noise and drinking in the yard. He said there were beer kegs, and that there was damage inside the house."

Joe looked down and the smile left his face. "Dad, I am real sorry."

"Give me the keys to your car now; get yourself a DART bus pass."

Joe reached into his pocket and handed me the keys before he turned and started to walk towards the house with his head down.

Maggie and I had not seen each other since the day I returned from the NCT in Arizona several months ago. I was a little bit apprehensive and didn't know what to expect. I walked through the front door and saw Maggie sitting in the living room.

"Hi Maggie, this is certainly a surprise, I didn't expect to see you again," I said.

Maggie smiled as she stood and walked over to me. "Lonny, nice to see you. I've missed you."

I didn't know what to say and started breathing hard. After a few seconds, I said, "Great to see you, Maggie."

We sat down next to each other on the couch and Maggie held both of my hands. "I made a big mistake leaving you and moving to Houston. My daughters only need to see me once a month, not every day. I missed you very much."

I looked into Maggie's eyes and said, "It's too bad you accepted the transfer to Houston."

Maggie briefly looked away and then turned to face me. "Well, I talked to my new boss and asked if I could run the Southwest Region out of the Dallas office. I told him I had to move back for personal reasons; if I couldn't then I was going to quit."

"What did he say?" I asked.

"He thought about it for a week and said that I could work out of the Dallas office if I came down to Houston for a couple of days every other week."

"That's fantastic," I said.

Maggie cocked her head to one side and smiled.

"Well, there's one problem...I sold my house."

"You could buy another one. Properties around here are always going on the market."

Maggie grinned. "I have another idea."

"What's that?" I asked.

"Your house is pretty big—what if I move in with you and Joe?"

We embraced and looked into each other's eyes for several moments. Then I said, "Maggie, that would be fantastic."

We started to kiss passionately on the couch and completely lost track of time and where we were. Several minutes must have passed before I heard a noise coming from the kitchen behind Maggie. Then I looked up and saw Joe. I wasn't sure how long he had been listening but he smiled and gave me a nod. I was hoping he would have the sense to go away but he stood there smiling and said, "Hey Dad, I need to go to the library tonight for a school project, can you give me a ride?"

The damn kid knew he had me in a box. I kept my left arm around Maggie and reached into my back pocket with my right hand to grab the car keys and tossed them to Joe. I shook my head, smiled and told Joe, "Get out of here!"

Joe looked at me and laughed as he walked out the front door.

THE END

ACKNOWLEDGMENTS

A heartfelt thank you to the many people who provided encouragement and feedback on several revisions during the last twelve months: Byron Beck, Robert Dees, Mabel Kung, Kevin Beck, Paul Beck, David Parham, Becky Hopson, Mike Twichell and two reviewers who wish to remain anonymous.

Michelle Josette provided an editorial review and copy edit. Her many suggestions significantly improved the novel. Gabriel Renfrow designed the cover. Pictures were provided by Brian Dunlap.

ABOUT THE AUTHOR

For most of his career, Philip has held leadership positions in finance, technology and analytics & optimization at two major airlines. In addition, he has done research and taught in academia.

For the last twelve months, he has spent all of his spare time writing his debut novel *Fastball*.

Philip lives in Dallas, Texas with his family.

.

CPSIA information can be obtained
at www.ICGtesting.com
Printed in the USA
LVOW03s1512110118
562712LV00001B/125/P